Tyrannia and Other Ren

Tyrannia and Other Renditions

Tyrannia and Other Renditions

Tyrannia and Other Renditions

Tyrannia and Other Renditions

Tyrannia
and
Other
Renditions

Alan DeNiro

Small Beer Press
Easthampton, MA

for Ally and Toby

This is a work of fiction. All characters and events portrayed
in this book are either fictitious or used fictitiously.

Small Beer Press
150 Pleasant Street #306
Easthampton, MA 01027
www.smallbeerpress.com
www.weightlessbooks.com
info@smallbeerpress.com

Distributed to the trade by Consortium.

Library of Congress Cataloging-in-Publication Data

DeNiro, Alan.
[Short stories. Selections]
Tyrannia and other renditions / Alan DeNiro. -- First edition.
    pages cm
ISBN 978-1-61873-071-8 (pbk. : alk. paper) -- ISBN 978-1-61873-072-5 (ebook)
I. Title.
PS3554.E5325A6 2013
813'.54--dc23
                                2013028987
First edition 1 2 3 4 5 6 7 8 9

Text set in Centaur.

Printed on 50# 30% PCR recycled Natures Natural paper by the Maple Press in York, PA.
Author photo © 2013 by Shelly Mosman (shellymosman.com).
Cover © 2013 by Kevin Huizenga (usscatastrophe.com/kh)

~~Renditions~~
~~Tyrannia~~
~~Politics~~
~~Consequences~~
Table of Contents

001 Tyrannia
009 A Rendition
027 Cudgel Springs
033 (*_*?) ~~~~ (-_-): The Warp and the Woof
063 Plight of the Sycophant
077 Dancing in a House
081 Highly Responsive to Prayers
093 Walking Stick Fires
111 The Flowering Ape
135 Moonlight Is Bulletproof
153 The Wildfires of Antartica
163 Tyrannia (II)
171 The Philip Sidney Game

Tyrannia

The man crashes to the ground, and then lies still, and birds fly to the site of him. They land on him from head to toe. He doesn't move, and won't move again of his own volition. In his arteries, though, are the beginnings of a journey.

Hands slap each other clean in the distance, and the sound moves away.

It took the man a long time to reach this moment. He had to fumble through decades of reality to reach this moment. Now, reality could not be his guide anymore. He had married young, had children—where are they now?—raised them, founded a school, grew flowers inside his house and bred horses outside of it, nursed a successful home-based business, buried his wife, dug her up to tell her one last thing, and buried her again. And then, nothing was important anymore. So he decided to become an agitator, to disturb the peace.

The birds are not at peace. The birds begin to equip themselves. They are making shadows on his bare torso with their wings. A rib juts out of his skin. A bluebird lands on the rib and perches there, as if overseeing the site, where the six other birds dance. They strut, lifting their skinny legs and talons high, posing for the sun that has at last shown its face in the valley.

Much is afoot. Preparations need to be made in the man's caves and tunnels. Treasures need to be inserted in opportune places: in the extremities at the ends of tunnels, and in the secret organs as well. Fortunes need to be pinpointed—they cannot be recognized piecemeal.

If the man knew that a sparrow was putting its beak inside the slit in his throat and regurgitating beetle larvae there, he might have been surprised, but not terrified. If the man knew that an egret was measuring the laceration on his broken leg, he would have been amused, but not forlorn. He always had a fondness for unruly birds when he agitated. In the public square of the city, where sorcerers frequently used to burn to death—not of their own volition—he would watch the flocks swirl like aerial litter, homing in on crumbs. The man would pause from his agitation, take a sip of water from his canteen, and watch them overtake the People's Fountain, skimming the water for insects. The water had a brown film on it, but lovers and children would still throw coins in the fountain, under the watchful eye of the emperor's soldiers. People would pass by him and ignore him. He had a book that he read from, *Of Clouds*, which explained a complicated system for the deliverance of justice and bread, which he liked to distill in easy-to-remember exclamations.

Even in those energetic days, it was hard for him to walk. At some point, he knew the body wouldn't function right ever again. Everything once done with ease would become heavy with pain and small steps would be triumphs. And then, even those small steps would become dreams. In the meantime, he tried to convince people that the structure of reality that passersby experienced was a carefully modulated illusion. The soldiers, at that time, considered him a meandering joke that hadn't quite reached its punchline, and maybe never would.

In that, they were onto something. A few bears come down into the valley, stepping over all the other bodies, to keep an eye on the site. At a safe distance. The birds could be testy in the middle of their site management, especially before their mid-morning tea. The bears have traveled quite a distance through ashen forests and dry riverbeds to reach this valley. They wish they were small enough like beetles to really get inside the man. The freshly hatched beetles, on the other hand, wish that they were as large as bears and could roam the countryside and really scare people. But they both realize, as if of mutual accord, that one doesn't always receive one's favored lot in life, and that in every loss there can be opportunity.

For example, the beetles imagine the man's bloodsystem to be a spectacular network of tunnels, which they lord over—though, really, they don't forget that the birds would always keep a watchful eye. They establish a base in the burst heart and set up defensive perimeters throughout the arterial system, depositing gold dung in strategic points that match the topography of the emperor's summer home. The birds twitter outside the body, clinking their tea cups together, which the beetles along the spine hear as brittle rumbles. And the beetles, in burrowing through the plasma, eat traces of the man's life, which they don't understand. But through the taste—iron, zinc, quicksilver—they gather a composite. Fresh quicksilver, recently cooled, poured into the mouth, cascading through the lake of the stomach and into the blood tunnels. But the words *no more, no more,* do they echo in the mercury? They do not. The man would not say those words, or the words, *I will tell you everything you want* or *Wait, wait . . . I will show you the safehouse, they will not expect you between the hours of three and four, and if you knock three times they will let you in the tunnel that leads from the outhouse to their map room.*

The man's compatriots didn't have a safehouse, but that is beside the point. Even if they did, the man wouldn't have spoken of it. He would have let the wind, chattering through the charcoaled pines outside the interrogation facility, do the speaking for him. With the quicksilver gurgling in his mouth, it would not have been enough to save him. The wind's words could not satisfy anyone, let alone a questioner. Who grew bored and decided to break the man's legs—no, break the legs and then puncture a hole in the rib cage, for starters, after the full application of quicksilver. The questioner's benevolent aides flipped through the manual. The man tried to look his questioner in the eye, but he wore a mask

of downy black gauze with no visible eye-slits. Plenty of precau-
tions were taken to prevent eye contact. While his legs were being
broken, the man thought of his compatriots, who had scattered
to the winds after the man was detained. The others were nothing special—neither was he—but they believed in ideas and the
illusory nature of the empire as well. They worked amongst the
poor—as they themselves were—and landscaped the courtyards
of administrators and baked bread for court scribes who they
tried to poison, rather unsuccessfully. But no matter. They liked
the man agitating in the public square. Many of them had gone
to trade school together, or worked in the same fields together,
or served in the same prisons for minor offenses together. They
decided to bring him into their disparate circles. What were they
going to do about the empire? That was unclear. The man tried
to talk about the book, *Of Clouds*, with the compatriots, but they
weren't sure of the proper prognosis from that book, and thus
moved onto other things. They grew together socially, which was
deemed necessary, in those trying times, to persevere through
the long days of the empire's zenith. They played a lot of bridge,
drank unlevied beer, and the more adventurous among them even
found themselves in mutual trysts, though the man himself was
too old for that. All the same, he didn't disapprove—in sorrow
there had to be love and in love, sorrow. The theory pleased him,
but became horribly fitting when, after one of these trysts went
sour, one of the estranged parties became a collaborator for the
empire. The empire, though it knew little of love, counted on
these betrayals.

At root, he and the collaborators were harmless. He knew no
one would believe that. Many of the collaborators have become even
more harmless, on account of their deaths, strewn in the same valley
where he resides. The empire has deposited many bodies in this
valley, about a half-mile walk from the capital city, through a narrow
riverbed road, piled high on each side with refuse, watched closely
by gray vultures (themselves birds who would never participate

4

in a site investigation, choosing instead to skulk and cherrypick the remains).

Out of all of those bodies in the valley, the birds see something site-worthy within the man, a joie de vivre in his broken nature. A hue, one which becomes even more apparent as the man starts to really come in his own. The secret organs are blossoming. A thorn grows out of the tip of his appendix, which the beetles circle. But even this is only a harbinger of the white rose, with a full arsenal of thorns, to burst out of that vestige. Tiny daisies spring from the roof of his mouth, which the beetles frolic amongst, upside down and clinging. And the birds, after their tea, have their imaginations captured by the bruised torpor of the man's skin. They lattice the exterior with their beaks, crushing berries and grapes against his chest for an autumn ointment. The egret mulches the grapes against his stomach with its feet, as if it is a supreme winemaker. Once the oil is prepared, the admixture is smeared across the body with their heads, the ointment seeping through the exterior into the unknown interior of bodily pastures and hideaways.

Now, the man knew, well before he was blindfolded and taken to the interrogation facility, that the empire also had its core bodily principles: every question needed an answer, no matter the absurdity of question. For his captors to think otherwise would be a desecration that had to be recorded on the body, in order to purify it. While his questioner would try to make him break, the man thought about the time before the empire, when men and women lived in karst caves and serpentine tunnels, and hunted the giant terror-birds with poisoned spears. When the intricate checks and balances of society were nonexistent. He had read somewhere that the emperor was an avid collector of terror-bird skulls, large as melons. Those birds had been hunted to extinction. He tried to think thoughtless thoughts. At night, shivering in his cell, he watched the moon turn the cloudless black sky into a dark blue. The moon forced the sky to drown the stars. And he laughed—though it hurt a lot—because he knew the stars, though drowned, would return. Moreover, the clouds would one day drown the moon. A few hours later he died from the cold. The jailor, charged with keeping him alive for several more weeks, was interrogated in the man's place. Despondent, the interrogation team sold the man's body and then realized he was the last of that ring of conspirators. They thought they had a couple more of his compatriots in the queue.

Through the mule ride, past the sourpuss surveillance of the vultures between the garbage cairns, the man didn't stir. The wagon drivers covered their mouths with white silk squares as they approached the valley. In spring, the valley would be swarming with flies, but in the dry winter air, there were only motley bird flocks visible, skittering above the amalgamation and merger of bodies. At the terminus of the road, the wagon drivers hoisted up the man's body, and on a heave of three, pitched him into the gorge. They slapped their hands clean. The dust settled and then wings' shadows appeared on the site of the man like gnomons.

After a time, though, the man's body becomes an ecology of many shadows. The birds use his breakages as terrain. His belly button has widened to a glade, with bamboo shoots along the water's edge sprouting upward from the intestines. The beetles ferment the organs. The man's site is full of what he left behind: glades, a ring of boulders on his thigh that used to be kidney stones, hoisted upward by beetles and plucked by the birds. And the jutting rib has petrified into a promontory overlooking the babbling pool.

The birds are somewhat satisfied but they rub their heads together, clean each other's feathers, and take a few deep breaths before starting on the cottage. With bone, with cartilage, they construct the foundation on, and as part of, the man's chest. When they are done, a pocket of air, long hidden inside the man's lungs, is released by the construction, and a draft rises up from the basement to the skeletal roof.

The emperor himself feels a slight tightness in his chest as he reads a novel by the fireplace, bearskin rugs at his feet, ensconced in his cottage as preparations are made for another wave of counter-insurgencies. The preparations are made in the capital, in the seat of government, far from the idylls of his retreat, with its glades, deep and contemplative limestone pools, delightful caves, rings of boulders, and crags arching out of the mildly tilled earth. He doesn't care much about the twinge's existence. They always pass like clouds. His novel is an adventure about a group of scientist-conquerors who come across a secret civilization on a remote island, far away from the tradewinds. They are surprised to find that the island denizens, powdered in gold, have been expecting them.

As he reaches that cliffhanger, he feels the tremor again in his body, and it's then clear that the vibrations are not coming from within his body, but rather from outside of it, outside of the cottage. But instead of beginning an investigation of the noise, he falls asleep there, the novel propped on his chest, hands folded on the novel. He snores as a trace of saliva trails down the corner of his mouth. And the sun sets over him and his dreams of terror-birds lording over the island jungles, and the necessary dreams of war that every emperor must have, which will terrify him—until, upon waking, they are forgotten.

As he sleeps, the sun sets over the thousands of corpses in the valley, of all shapes and sizes, which now surround the cottage. Or rather, the cottage has arrived to be surrounded by the bodies. Bodies that used to be mothers, fathers, sons, and daughters are on every compass point around the cottage, bodies that, when they had working mouths and voices, had given the wrong answers to the wrong questions. The emperor keeps sleeping though, as the wind rustles through their rags. He keeps sleeping through the squawking of birds as they begin their flight from the site that the emperor's cottage now inhabits—scraping their talons on the slate of the cottage's roof. He sleeps as the bears amble away, on a journey back to the land where the trees have leaves and needles and smell good. It's a long journey.

And underneath the cottage, the man is in the soil, no longer having what he used to have. The beetles are carrying his secret breath and dreams throughout the valley. And all the beetles are dreaming the same dream as they burrow. They are dreaming of the emperor, how he will waken right before sunrise—from that smell, what is that smell—and look out the window in the drowsy gray to see what the sun will bring.

A Rendition

Patrick was a key component of their plan. His first order of business was cleaning out his mom's minivan. His mom was at a business conference somewhere warm. He parked the minivan in the driveway and opened the liftback. He then removed the boxes of his mom's sales brochures, his sister's field hockey equipment, and a wasteland of empty pop cans and potato chip bags. It was clammy and cold outside. After putting all of the junk down in the garage and throwing the trash away, he ran the cord for the vacuum cleaner to the minivan and gave the whole van a good cleaning, and then sprayed the fabric down with Febreze. The plan didn't need the fresh scent of "Mountain Rain" to work, but he still wanted to make sure the van didn't smell bad for the rendition.

He was feeling well-rested and ready, in the middle of a week of unpaid leave of absence. He was a custodian for the university where he used to study, where the professor taught. His supervisors were more than glad to give him the leave; he hoped he would have a job when he came back.

After he finished and parked the van in the garage again, Tristana called him. Tristana was his ex-girlfriend, though they were still on good terms. They had to be, in order to fulfill the plan. She was in the paralegal program in the university—where he used to study, before he got kicked out—and worked as an administrative assistant in the law school. More important, she worked two offices down from the professor.

"Yeah, so." Tristana sighed. "How do you feel?"

"Fine, I guess."

"Are you feeling angry about the professor? Rageful? I mean, you're not going to let your emotions get in the way of things?"

"I don't think so," Patrick said. For him, executing the plan was never that much about a sense of righteous anger. Sure, there was an abstract belief in a just cause, and in a way he was afraid of the professor, though the professor himself, aside from his ideas, posed little threat. And he wasn't even really afraid of getting caught. Instead, the plan for him was a form of self-discovery, to throw himself into a project that would define who he was. Doing this, he would see himself in a different light.

"Good," Tristana said. "I think of emotions as little as possible. They really cloud things."

"Yeah."

"Okay, we'll meet at your place at dawn—uh, that's 5:57. Got that?"

"Got it—oh shit."

"What?"

"I forgot to tape up the windows of the minivan."

"Well you better get on that. I gotta fill out some briefs now. Later."

"Later."

When he was in line at Walgreens with the tape, he got a call from Evan, who was the bona fide leader of their group. He was a real anarchist. He went to a lot of protests with bags of blood to throw at police. He had been arrested seven times and Patrick wondered if he was sleeping with Tristana.

"How are you feeling?" Evan said.

"Tristana asked me the same thing."

"She would. We're like, one mind," he said. Then, "We're all like one mind."

"Uh-huh. I feel fine by the way." He fumbled in his pocket for a dime to finish paying for the duct tape. The woman behind him with two kids pulling at her knees rolled her eyes. She would never know about the plan. And the cashier giving him the receipt and the bag with the duct tape would never know about the plan.

"What, you going zen on me?" Evan said. He said zen like it was a curse word. "I don't want you to feel 'fine.' You have to, you know, listen to your heart. And your heart should be fucking pissed." Evan and the static on his end intertwined, as if the hissing interference was coming from his throat.

"Okay," Patrick said. "Listen. I'm angry. You can't hear it on the phone, but I am."

"Patrick, this is going to be great," Evan said. "It's going to be a fun weekend. The farmhouse, it's nice. It's really nice. I have a ton of beer too."

"That's good," Patrick said, though he didn't know if he would be in the mood for getting wasted while executing the plan.

"Okay, look, I have to go," Evan said in a slightly exasperated tone, as if Patrick was the one who had called him. "I have to print out the manual at the copy shop."

"Great, see you tomorrow."

Evan hung up and Patrick laughed as he started up the van.

Back in his driveway, he got to work on the windows. The air was still damp, so he wasn't sure if he was getting a good seal with the duct tape on the window. And the tape was clinging to the newspaper. After about a half hour, he got all of the back windows taped up with the newspaper. He tossed the duct tape roll onto the front seat. They would need more of that later. He lay in the back for a few minutes, watching the translucent light filter through the news of the world and its ads. Only the ads for flat-screen televisions would not let the light sift through, black rectangles like those monoliths from *2001*. At last, he closed his eyes. He was excited. He was starting to feel something.

"Is that Febreze?" Evan said while Patrick was driving the van.

"Yeah," Patrick said. Evan was wearing his black bandana over his nose and mouth, so Patrick wasn't sure how he could smell anything.

"It's nice. Really nice."

They were on the outskirts of town, past the last outposts of the higher-end outlet malls. Patrick was driving the van well within the legal speed limit. Evan and Tristana were in the back seat, and the professor was lying down in the back-back. The duct tape, the interrogation manual, and their box of clothes and sundries were riding shotgun. Evan's uncle's old farmhouse was about fifteen minutes away.

The professor started flailing around and mumbling.

"Hey, hey," Evan said. "Sit." He leaned over the seat and beat the professor on the shoulder blade with his billy club a few times. The professor screamed, though the duct tape muffled most of the sound. Tristana laughed, and ran her hand through Evan's stringy braids. Patrick turned his attention back to the road. He would have thought that the minivan might have attracted more attention on campus, but on Monday morning there were few students and workers around. The execution of the first part of the plan was flawless.

"I have your dossier in the front seat here," Evan said. "You're, like, a fucking monster."

The professor bucked his head around. His glasses flew off his face, underneath the seat.

"Whoa, you'll break your glasses, professor," Tristana said. She leaned down and fished under the seat for the glasses. Patrick watched her from his rearview mirror and saw her T-shirt ride up. He saw the tattoo on her lower back—a series of Sumerian cuneiforms that she told him was the ancient word for freedom—for the first time since they broke up. Tristana found the glasses, folded them, and put them in her purse.

There was a long honk outside and the flash of a white roofing van. The van was inches away from the window.

"Jesus, Patrick, you ran that stop sign!" Evan said.

The other van stopped, and then sputtered forward in the intersection again.

Patrick wasn't sure whether to slow down more or speed up.

"Sorry, sorry," Patrick said, his face flush. He sped up. "That sign . . . it wasn't there a couple weeks ago."

He knew the excuse was itself incompetent.

"What the fuck would have happened . . ." Evan began, but Tristana put a hand on his shoulder.

"It's okay, Evan. No harm, no foul."

Evan sighed and then leaned over the seat. "What do you think professor? What is your expert opinion? No harm, no foul?"

The professor didn't say anything, and couldn't say anything. The one-way banter continued until they reached the farmhouse, but Patrick didn't pay attention to any of it, focusing on the road with the efficiency of a vice.

The farm was desolate, set in a sloping valley with an abandoned apple orchard. Evan said that there were limestone caves underneath the main house. His great-great uncle had mined a tunnel that connected the storm basement to those caves. "No one knows where they end," Evan had said in one of their planning sessions in Tristana's flat. No one had lived at the farm for ten years, and in that time, the house and the other buildings had fallen into severe disrepair. The front porch of the house sagged and bowed. The front door was ripped off and an upside-down lawn tractor blocked the gap. The grain silo, shorn of its shingles, looked like a stone obelisk from an interplanetary civilization. The barn's paint was fading, and many of the fence posts on the property had been knocked over or driven over.

"We're home," Evan said. "Park outside the barn."

Patrick parked there and the three of them got out. Evan opened the back hatch and yanked at the professor's collar, pulling him out and to the ground.

"Black site," Evan said. "Black site. You are now leaving the United States of America. You are in the Kingdom of Tyrannia now." He pulled down his bandana for a second and scratched his nose. "You are not a citizen here. You don't have any rights here, on account of the accords that our country has signed with the underworld. Do you understand?"

The professor looked up at him and said nothing.

Evan laughed. "All right, all right. I'm throwing a lot at you. Come on." He took the professor by the shoulder and helped him up, almost helpfully. The professor complied. Evan had come up with the name of Tyrannia during one of their brainstorming sessions. Patrick felt like he was watching a movie on DVD, with a bored director's commentary having a distant opinion on whatever they were doing. *We chose the farmhouse on account of the caves. It was a great set. A great set. Uh, and we knew the professor would be scared there . . .*

"Patrick can you get the stuff in the front seat?" Tristana said. She had put the professor's glasses on her forehead.

"Sure." *What was Patrick's motivation? Well, that's a good question. He took a class with the professor—a long time ago—and that's why he was expelled, because he plagiarized his first paper in the class . . . uh, I think it was on the separation of powers . . .*

"Thanks." She gave him a warm smile that he knew was manipulation, but he didn't care. He took the box and shut the door with the back of his heel. As he went up the stairs, Tristana called out from inside the house, "Watch out for that last step. You'll fall through." Patrick edged around the step and then the upside-down tractor. He could hear the other three in the basement. The living room had been a hideout for local kids with BB guns, beer, and huffing addictions—targets taped up on the walls with bull's-eyes blasted through on the outlined heads, breasts, and groins; shattered bottles of MGD littering the floor; glue canisters. In the kitchen there was a twenty-year-old snowmobile and the oven was ripped out. He went down the stone stairs, and the air changed from being rancid to something colder and cleaner.

In the basement, Tristana and Evan were preparing the site. The professor was sitting Indian style on the dirt floor. He was coughing. Patrick set the materials down. In one of the corners he could see a natural archway and a dark opening, which must have been one of the tunnels that Evan talked about.

"Aha," Tristana said, finding the pliers in the box underneath a bag of SunChips. She twirled them on her finger like a six shooter. "There they are."

"Okay, remember," Evan said, rubbing his hands together and standing over the professor. Everyone's breath was visible. "The point of this exercise is to, you know, gather relevant information about what he knows." He took a chair from the corner and scraped it to the center of the room. Tristana hoisted the professor onto the chair. The professor was tipping.

"Don't fall over," she said. "Shit, Ev, do you think we should tie him to the chair?"

"Hmm," Evan said. "Then we would have to cut his hands free. I don't know."

"What does it say in the manual?" Tristana said.

"Right." Evan sifted through the box that Patrick had brought in and found the Interrogation Manual. "Uh, shit," he said to the professor. "You should know. You wrote this, didn't you?"

"I don't think he wrote it," Tristana said. "He wrote the legal memos for the Department of Justice that allowed the manual to come into being."

"Yeah, yeah, I know," Evan said, looking peeved. "It was, I don't know, a grandiose metaphor." He turned to Patrick. "How about you bring down the cooler of beer that I brought here yesterday? It should still be cold."

Patrick hesitated. "Sure, where is it?"

"By the door, I think." Evan had already turned back to the manual. Tristana ripped off the duct tape covering the professor's mouth, and he screamed. The noise was muffled by the walls.

Patrick's face was hot as he went up the stairs. Evan's attitude and his commands were really beginning to get to him. Evan wasn't recognizing the role that Patrick had in the plan, or that they were all a small society of equals. And wasn't that harmony the *point* of the plan? Patrick had first come up with the idea of the plan. He would have to say something at some point to Evan—and Tristana. He found the cooler by the fireplace, not by the door as Evan had said, and took a beer from it. After the second beer, he saw Tristana standing in front of him.

"What the fuck are you doing?" she said.

He shrugged and stood up from the cooler. "I'm just bringing this downstairs."

"Yeah, like, an hour later," she said. "You need to stop pouting, Patrick. This is very stressful for Evan."

"Evan? That's who you're worried about?"

"A little." She took one of the beers from the cooler, took a few swallows, and wiped her mouth with her sleeve. "He's under a lot of pressure."

"We all are."

"No, no . . ." She bit her lip and actually looked thoughtful. "Are you the one doing the interrogation? Are you down there?"

"No, he's ordering me around like a lackey."

"It's for your own protection. Look, the professor . . . he thought, for years, that he could get away with what he did, you know? That he could lead a normal life after crafting the legal framework for all of those black sites, and see his family every night and tuck his children in at night. All while innocent people were being plucked from their homes all across the world. That's what kind of monster we're dealing with." She finished the rest of her beer. "Evan's down there with the manual—the manual that the professor advised on and signed off on—and he's going to get more names. Places. Valuable information. You and I, we need to do our jobs and be there for Evan."

"And what are we going to do with this information then?"

"Evan knows people in a lot of networks. All around the world."

Patrick picked up the cooler. "So what's your job then? Fucking him?" He couldn't believe that he had said that, but was actually kind of relieved when he did.

"Fuck you," Tristana said. She tossed the beer can against the targets and went down the stairs.

"I thought you were supposed to control your emotions," Patrick called out after her.

What upset him more, though, was that after he went downstairs again—something which he was thinking about not doing—Tristana and Evan barely paid him any mind. Evan cocked his head a little to indicate where Patrick should set down the cooler, but he was putting the professor in a stress position and didn't want his concentration broken. Tristana was flipping through the manual and then held out the book for Evan to read, like an assistant turning the sheet music for a concert pianist. Evan took off the professor's pants. The professor was gritting his teeth. His gag was off.

"I . . . I . . ." he started to say.

Tristana perked up. "What was that? It's okay. You can tell us."

"This is ridiculous," the professor blurted out. Patrick restrained a laugh, though he wasn't sure what was funny.

Evan spat on the floor and paced around the professor. Patrick knew he was performing for Tristana more than the professor. And Tristana obliged; her eyes followed Evan and only Evan.

"It *is* ridiculous," Evan said. "Because we know you know. You have to tell us what everyone knows—from the president on down."

The professor shook his head.

"Tristana, give me those pliers," Evan said. Tristana gave him the pliers. Evan took in his other hand a bucket of water that was in the corner.

He said: "So does that manual say to douse him with the cold water and then pull off his fingernails or . . ."

"Let me check," Tristana said, wetting her finger and flipping through. "It's like they use code words for all of the different techniques," she said. "Euphemisms. It's hard to keep them straight."

"See, if I get him wet I might not be able to get a good grip on the fingernails," Evan said. "There has to be a proper order of these things."

"It's not a cookbook," Patrick said, but no one paid attention to him. He got himself another beer and downed it quickly.

"Aw, fuck it," Evan said, pouring the water over the professor. "We'll let you stew for a little bit. Then you can tell us everything you know." The professor shivered and tried to shake the water off.

"I need a break," Evan said, pulling down his bandana. He rummaged through his jacket pocket for cigarettes, and lit, pacing and smoking. Tristana leaned against the wall, her arms crossed, staring with boredom at the professor.

"My uncle," Evan said between drafts of the cigarette, "he was a weird guy. I liked him. He didn't take shit from anybody."

"Okay," Patrick said, not sure where this was going. The professor was really shivering.

"He told us kids we could never go in the tunnels because people would get lost down there. And never come back. It was actually the only advice I ever listened to, from any blood relations."

"Why is that?" Patrick said, actually curious.

Evan smiled. "Because he said he'd kill me if I ever thought about going in the tunnels, and I believed him. He had a dishonorable discharge from Nam. You." He flicked his cigarette at the professor. The cigarette, cinder-first, bounced off his forehead, but he didn't pay it any attention. He kept shivering instead. "Did you ever serve there? I didn't think so. Anyway, my uncle was pretty messed up from the war. I miss him a lot."

Tristana went over and took Evan's hand. Patrick cringed, and then hoped neither of his friends saw it. But they didn't say anything. Tristana kept squeezing Evan's hand and he had a wistful look on his face. When he looked sad, he didn't look like a revolutionary at all. Or maybe a different kind of revolutionary, one that posed for glorious paintings back when people did those kinds of things.

"Come on, Tristana," Evan said, putting his arm around her. "I . . . I need to refocus."

"Patrick," Tristana said with a smile. "Make sure that he doesn't escape." Then she and Evan went up the stairs. Patrick could hear them both laughing. He imagined that she would tell him, while she straddled him on the cot in the living room, that Patrick was being a jealous prick and maybe they shouldn't have trusted him at all, and Evan would have shrugged, unlistening, tracing his hands on the phoenix tattoo on her chest, a tender gesture that he would conjure at times. The professor coughed and Patrick blinked and turned to him. But the professor's head sank down again.

Patrick walked to the professor and stood in front of him. "Look at me," he said. "Look at me."

The professor looked up at him. Patrick tried to say something like Evan would have said, something cutting, but nothing came to him.

"Do you know they were talking about you when you were upstairs?" the professor said, teeth chattering. The professor smelled like an untended fish tank.

Patrick shook his head. "Tell me what they said."

The professor shrugged. Then he said, "Tyrannia . . ."

"I don't have time for this," Patrick said. He scooped up another beer and went up the stairs, but quietly, so that Evan and Tristana wouldn't hear him. But he could hear them laughing softly. They weren't paying any attention to Patrick. He went outside. It was raining. The fog rolled over the fields of buckwheat and thistle, and the dying apple trees. He stood on the porch and drank his beer. The plan was not going as he had thought it would.

"Fuck it," he said. He tossed the half-full beer can toward the barn, where it spun in a shower of watery gold. Then he walked to the van, thinking that at any moment Evan would come out with his pants half on and say *Where the fuck do you think you're going*, but he didn't. Patrick got in, put the van in neutral and coasted backward down the hill. At the bottom he started it up and did a three-point turn. He looked at the farmhouse and the barn and the mist rising up the hill toward the barn and then gunned the minivan down the narrow road.

He took a couple of wrong turns, sat in the parking lot in an abandoned gas station, trying to retrace his steps, wondering how to get home. Driving again, Patrick thought about Evan's story about his uncle, and whether anyone had a similar influence in his own life. No one came to mind. No teacher, no relative, no mentor, no crossing guard. Maybe Tristana. That was the only person he could possibly think of. But that was long past over. He felt saddened by this for about a second or two—the time for his heart to beat a couple of times—and then he was filled with an overwhelming sense of relief.

When he finally made it back, it was getting dark. There wasn't any fog in town. The lights were on; his mom must have taken a taxi back. He stripped the back windows of the newspaper and peeled off the duct tape. He checked the minivan's carpet for blood—miraculously, there was none. His mom was in the living room watching *Deal or No Deal*.

"Hey hon," she said. Patrick kissed her on the forehead.

"Hey mom," he said. "How was the trip?"

"Oh, fine. Work left a message, they want to know if you can work a double on your first day back."

"Okay. I'm going to lie down now."

"What have you been up to?"

Patrick shrugged. "Thanks for letting me borrow the van."

"No problem, sweetie."

"Okay, I'll see you later mom."

"Love you sweetie."

"Love you too."

In his room, all he could think about was the professor's face, and his nonchalant shrug. He checked his email and went through all of Tristana's old messages, and Evan's old messages, and deleted them. He expected the FBI, or ATF, or whomever, to burst down his door, and wake his mother on the couch, and force her to the floor at gunpoint, and charge up the stairs. He was ready for the plan to end like that. But there was no commotion as he had imagined it. He fell asleep with the lights on.

He had no dreams, only the darkness of sleep, when his cell phone woke him up, vibrating and chirping on his nightstand. It was four in the morning. His lamp was still on and the house was quiet. He picked up the phone; Tristana was calling him. He let it ring three times, staring at her name, and then flipped his phone open.

"Hello?" he said.

The connection wasn't good, but he could tell she was breathing heavily.

"Hello? Tristana?"

After a few seconds she finally talked. "Patrick," she whispered. "You have to come back. Oh . . ." Her mouth moved away from the phone; he could hear her voice, panicked, and another more distant voice, as well as a rumbling sound. "Oh God . . . please come back. You have to help us. I can't . . ."

"Do you know what time it is?" Patrick said.

"Time?" she said. "Are you talking about time?"

Another voice in the distance, a high wail.

"Is the FBI there?" he said. "Is this a trap?"

"I forgive you," she said. "Of course, of course I forgive you. And I'm sorry too. I made a lot of mistakes, Patrick. But it's almost too late . . . please come. The tunnel—"

Then he lost the signal. He tried calling her back, but he couldn't even get her voicemail, only a recorded message that a connection was not possible at that time. He sat up in bed, arms crossed, biting his lip, wondering what possibilities were really before him. The whole day was beginning to sink into him. Then the phone rang again. It was an unlisted number.

"Hello?" Patrick said.

There was nothing at first, then a low-pitched hum. It might or might not have been one of the sounds he heard when Tristana called him. The sound increased in pitch and intensity and then the connection died. He stared at the phone and flipped it off.

"Shit," he said. He felt like he should have been scared or something. But he knew he wouldn't have padded down the stairs and out of the house to the van if he was scared.

More than anything, he wanted to see Tristana's face.

A few more wrong turns on country roads of mist, white darkness in his headlights and branches scraping against the side of the van. He felt drunk still. The mountain rain Febreze lingered in the van like a hospital's spoor. When lost, he spun the van out on muddy parking lots connected to no buildings, in order to turn around and retrace his path. Outside of town, he only passed one other car, which weaved in the road so much that Patrick waited on the berm for the car to pass, its honks receding in the distance.

After a few false starts, he finally found his way and his memory reasserted itself. At the foot of the farmhouse hill, he tried to keep his hands from shaking. There were no lights in the house and no other vehicles parked outside. There weren't crickets. He climbed the hill and parked right in front of the house. He left the headlights on, took a flashlight in one hand and a baseball bat in the other, and got out of the van. No sounds. As he stepped into the house, the headlights did more harm than good. In the living room, the mattress was still there, with a twin depression in the middle.

"Hello?" he called out. "Tristana?"

He stood at the top of the stairs. There was a dim light coming from down there. He slowly went down the stairs, darting his flashlight around and finding nothing to see.

On the basement floor, the battery-powered lamp was almost dead, giving off a reddish glow. The cooler was overturned and crushed beer cans were scattered everywhere. In the center of the room, the chair was still there—though its legs looked burnt and scorched—and was empty except for the professor's shoes on the seat, polished black. The leather captured the glow from the lamp like the clouds of a dark Jupiter. Feathery strands of rope, like pillow down, were scattered around the chair. The rest of the basement was empty, but he did hear a trickling from the archway opening in the far corner. He took a deep breath and walked to the opening.

A blast of cold air. He crossed his arms. He took a few steps into the tunnel, which began to slope downward. The footing was slick. He looked at his own sneakers and wondered if he was going to slide down the rest of the way. As he tried to grip the rough stone wall, his flashlight slipped out of his hands and skittered down the slope for a few seconds until it stopped.

"Shit," he said. The sound didn't echo; it died.

He heard sloshing down below. He stopped himself from sliding any farther and held his breath.

Someone picked up the flashlight, and flicked it around, revealing a cavern about as large as the basement above, filled with a couple inches of reddish water. The person was all shadows until putting the flashlight under the chin. It was Tristana. She had a black eye, lacerations on the cheeks, torn clothes, gray skin. She was also barefoot.

"Tristana," Patrick whispered. "Come on up. Come on. I found you." He kept himself from rushing down to her. It was not a hard decision and that surprised him.

She looked up at Patrick but didn't seem to recognize him. She wiggled the flashlight around the cavern walls, as if she hadn't ever used one before. Patrick could catch glimpses of human skeletons and bear skulls embedded on the rough walls below him.

"Tristana!" he said.

More footsteps, and someone took the flashlight away from Tristana. It was Evan. He was hunched over. He was carrying the professor on his back, who looked unconscious or dead. Evan looked as mottled and wounded as Tristana did. He was barefoot also, and didn't have any fingernails. He looked up at Patrick too, and then past him. Then Evan dropped the flashlight and they both turned away from the light and kept moving until Patrick couldn't hear their footsteps anymore.

Patrick stumbled back the way he came. The light was turning gray in the east. His headlights were dimming, and they would have died if he had stayed down there any longer.

No one ever asked him any questions about the disappearances. He wanted someone to. He wanted to be put through the ringer, to be placed in a small cell and asked penetrating questions about his role in the disappearance of three people. He wanted to be roughed up a little bit.

The university held memorial services. The Attorney General spoke at the funeral of the professor. Patrick avoided everything, and then went back to work waxing floors and making windows upon the quad sparkle. He tried to forget about the farmhouse, and the tunnels. Evan, Tristana, and the professor were a little harder to forget, but he was working on it. His dreams were dark spaces, and he liked it that way.

About two weeks after the funerals, he was watching TV alone on a Sunday night. His mother was out at a bar, and he tried not to think of the fact that she had more of a social life than he did. He was drifting off. The doorbell rang. Startled, it took him a few seconds to register the sound. It rung again, and he muttered to himself as he opened the door.

Tristana pushed open the door the rest of the way and came into the house, with Evan close behind her. The professor was still draped onto his back.

"Whew," Tristana said. "Glad we found you."

Their skin was grayer than before, with red scars and welts all over their bodies. Their clothes were tatters, and Tristana was almost naked. The professor's scalp was almost gone and Patrick could see a nest of black ovals at the base of his neck—beetles.

"Been looking everywhere for you, my man," Evan said. Tristana took Patrick's hand and squeezed it. Her hand felt like a cantelope that had been left in the icebox for months.

Evan hobbled over to the kitchen table and pulled out a chair, spilling a stack of bills and newspapers that were on the seat. Tristana sank down to the couch, still holding onto Patrick's hand. "Sit with me," she said, and Patrick sat next to her. She smelled like the monkey cages in the psychology building that Patrick had to sometimes clean. Evan deposited the professor onto the chair and flexed his shoulder blades. A few beetles dropped from his back onto the floor and scurried away. The professor moaned a little bit, though it might have been Evan throwing his voice. Tristana stroked Patrick's cheek.

"We, all of us, are together at last, my little bear," she said, and then she kissed him. He didn't want his heart to open up, or his mouth, but they did, and he kissed her back, crushing her tongue against his and licking the salty pulp, feeling her breathe like she was choking, and her neck quiver as if she was in danger. He was getting feverish, and at the same time his skin prickled all over with chills, but he didn't care. He kissed the giant scar on Tristana's forehead and then they settled into the couch to watch Evan work.

Evan slapped the professor's cheek, which gouged open. Then he took hold of Patrick's baseball bat, which was propped up against the kitchen table. Evan coughed a few times, and spat magnolias of blood onto the floor.

"Now," Evan said to the professor, "for the last time, tell me everything you know!"

Spring Cudgel

Things aren't working out too well here, are they? Or is it aren't they. You'll find out soon enough. Looks like there's a train here. Let go of my hand, now. Now! My train of thought leads upstate, to your camp. It's good you're going. It's a good camp. I'll try to impart some advice in these few minutes we have left together.

For starters, it helps to dress like everyone else and speak like your friends. Or don't speak at all if that floats your boat. Which is easier if you don't have friends. It's not advised where you are going. Finding friends, that is. I know this, I lurked there in my salad days. Don't self-edit, but avoid embarrassment. Don't assume everyone is staring at you because you're crazy. You might be crazy, but that's probably not why they're staring at you. There are beasts in the old growth forest where you are going, and not all of them are quadrupeds. I've packed Deep Woods Off. It could help. What we're talking about is honesty. An honesty in assessing situations you don't understand.

I'm trying to wipe that frown off your face. Maybe you should take my pulse. But be sure to return it as soon as you're done with it. That's funny. I like staring at depressed people. I wonder if they think of me ever. But then I go to work. Oh, work works me into a frenzy. There's this game I play. I print out hundreds of pages when the printer is low on toner. How long can I go before anyone says anything? I guestimate displeasure. You must be thinking: so kill an octopus and be done with it, already! But then it's 5. The money grows on the money tree and I pluck some off every two weeks. Which allows for your room and board and your gratitude. Your father might think differently about this. I've also packed peanuts, grapes, and a mallet. If you really want "PB&J," as the supermarket calls it, you can do with these tools what you will. That type of food doesn't exist at the camp. You will doubtless be sleeping inside a cabin that used to be a concession stand.

Don't assume I'm taking you down a peg for the sake of it. For pity's sake. The gap between loving you and wanting you to be happy—there is a difference, do not doubt me—is one I travel through every day. It's more of a gulch. Sometimes I think it would be much easier if I were in a cult. A good countryside cult, where I could wear robes and raise legumes. It would help my complexion. Don't you think? Is my skin cold? Take my hand again. Nobody's watching. Ignore them!

When I was a girl—your look reminded me of something—I wanted a sawed off shotgun. I liked the way holding one sounded. Ideally, I would have received it as a gift. They say the same thing about tarot cards—better to be given a deck or steal one rather than buy one. The first was out of the question. The shotgun I stole was your grandfather's, no problem, he had plenty of shotguns and it wasn't as if he'd miss just one. I think you'd remember him from the sanatorium. There was a woodshed in our acreage. I commenced sawing there. But I wasn't sure where on the barrel to saw. This happened on a Sunday. I was without skill, being your age, and my hand slipped. The left pinky finger gashed on the saw tooth. As it turned out, the gun was also loaded, which was unfortunate. When I fell, the trigger kicked back and that finger blew right off like dandelion seeds. This was bigger than a mere scratch. I know this is a surprise to you, because of the verisimilitude of this finger I'm holding in front of you. Plastics make it probable. When Dad came in the woodshed for his nightly libations, he found me under his workbench and after the surgery I was on a train to Camp Cudgel Springs.

This is a lot to digest. Okay, you can let go again. You've warmed me up nicely. Look at the Snoopy backpack I got for you. Be sure to try it on before you need to run, such as from a serial killer who approaches your cabin. Not that I think that will happen. Or maybe he will only want a glass of water. You don't really have a "kill me, eat me" face. Camp changed my life as it will change yours. I was the youngest there, as you will be. This is healthy. See the parallels? Our lives are two rails, side by side, holding a loco-motive in place. On the first day at camp I tried to run away. I had a clever plan. I made a map with a stick on the ground, choosing a certain black ant that seemed to be of independent spirit to rep-resent me. The ant didn't follow my escape route, however, so I liberated it and took a nap, eschewing dinner. When everyone was asleep, I stole away from my noxious bunkmates into the woods. The trees were hundreds of years older than me. I didn't know their names and still don't. You'll have to choose, once you're there, whether to name them, although there's always the risk you'll run out of names. My clothes smelled like chicken strips. From the mess hall. Pay attention. I was afraid of predators picking up my chicken strip scent, naturally, so I decided to wash my clothes in the eponymous spring before making my way to the closest state highway. It would also help with the whole bloodhound issue.

(Regarding the spring, yes. Yes, it has had a troublesome his-tory. According to the legend depicted in the camp brochure, fifty Indians were massacred there. With their own hatchets. By Ameri-can forces. The Indians were supposedly going to poison the water, and were duly surrounded and taken care of, making the entire three-county area safe for habitation. What really happened—besides the massacre itself, of course—was anyone's guess. Motives are hard to discover unless a person is within sight, and under close observation. I'm standing right in front of you, so we're covered.)

I scrambled down the Hatchet Trail, into the gully—it might have been a gulch—at the base of which the spring resided. I could hear it gurgling during my descent. I can hear it gurgle now. Some day you might be able to. In moonlight I saw my face. I held up my four-fingered hand to the reflection. Suddenly my face didn't seem so interesting. Seeing an opportunity, I unrolled the little ice pack that I brought with me, which I had nurtured over the previous two weeks, and threw the remainders of my pinky into the spring. I wasn't sure if I was consecrating the finger or the spring. I kept what I could after the accident and that's a good rule of thumb. Just in general.

No phantasms chastised me or beat me up near the spring. No Indian ghosts were released from the water. I washed my clothes, but then, indeed, a quorum of camp counselors entered my sight line. I saw their peppy flashlights first, then their authoritarian rescue blazers. My bunkmate had had a nightmare about me, apparently. That was the tip off. When people have visions about you, and choose to act on them—tactically, I mean—you need to understand where they're coming from. In that they have no idea where they're coming from.

I waded into the water, which came up to my waist and was glacial. I raised my hands up and told them that I meant no harm, please don't kill me. I wasn't trying to poison the water.

I don't remember what they said back to me. I learned how to be less daring upon my return. I arched. I crafted dioramas out of bark and acorns and insect shells and broken lightbulbs and the discarded fingernails of my peers. I purchased souvenirs of my time at camp—false arrowheads, a tableau of the sunlight breaking through the forest canopy and shining upon the spring—and sent them back to my father with platitudes and euphemisms, which were codes for the untold anguish he had caused me. You wouldn't understand the souvenirs; they were from a bygone era.

Well, the conductor is flagging us. All right. I wish a company would manufacture a jacket that would protect you from wolves. The wolf packs have made a comeback. Not in our state, but you never know. Be sure to read the pamphlet I put in your backpack. You might acquire "tips" during your stay. You'll have plenty of time to practice tips while you wonder: why am I here? It's a legitimate question. I don't hate you, really, for thinking it.

Cudgel Springs was quaint. But once the spring dried up, it no longer seemed appropriate to stick to tradition for the sake of it. So the camp changed, in that it was abandoned. No kayaks, no crafts, no songs, no counselors. Just woods and buildings that age like we do. The trees are still tall and quiet. They tower over the Hatchet Trail, as well as the crater at the end of the trail. It's off-limits. A few years ago, foolish children from the nearby town—doubtless the descendants of the original settlers—went exploring in the woods near the crater and never came back. I saw it covered locally. Don't go there. The food's all frozen and in your pack. It should last you about a week, but after that you may have to forage. Do not worry about me. I want you to stop thinking of me. I'm sure that once you are there, others will come. Peers and counselors. You are my preemptive strike, my pioneer. If they do come, all of the other campers will come from better families than ours.

But they won't know what to expect.

So be keen, already. Don't write back if you're not going to be honest.

Wait, come back.

(and the Warp*?)
(and the Woof*?)

Roger found the notebook in his attic, tucked in the side pocket of a Kevlar jacket. The notebook contained his first novel, the one he wrote when he was twenty-two and never had the heart to revise, or learn any more about. He had forgotten about it, but the smell of his old cologne on the pages awakened his memory. The world that he had written about was long dead, but he wanted someone else to sift through the notebook, to extract something marketable from it. Roger couldn't read his own handwriting anymore. He stared and stared at it—the squiggles—but did anyone know cursive anymore? No one had penmanship. For a few delusional seconds he wondered whether someone else had written it.

He went downstairs. Having no luck figuring out what to do with the notebook, and too afraid to place it with his current material, next to his laptop (which still needed to be hand-cranked for the night), he called his agent, voice only.

"I'm going to ship the notebook to you, I mean manually." Above Roger was a framed picture of Roger with the president. Roger's hair was darker then—no, not the radiation, that had no effect on the color.

"What time is it?" his agent said.

"It's noon," Roger said. "What are you doing? Why are you still sleeping?"

The agent said nothing. The agent knew Roger didn't want to hear about Lord Manhattan, the sweeps and declarations. The agent would have moved out of Queens if she could but she didn't have the right IDs. The agent had to conduct meetings at night, and daytime security was expensive.

"Well," Roger said, after the pause, "okay, could you look at it, then? Maybe there's something there that could be extracted from it?"

"Sure, sure," the agent said, turning over, squinting at the blinds.

It took five business days for the notebook to reach the agent. FedEx lost a few planes in a flurry of SAMs the week before. Flight schedules were blown up and reconstructed. The courier who handed the package to the agent came at 3 a.m.

"Hang on, let me find my wand," the agent said, fumbling in her pockets. "Shit, do you have yours?"

The courier shook her head. "Sorry, mine got stolen."

"Just give me the package then. I can scan it later."

The courier shook her head, and eyed the corridor of the agent's building, the cameras like rifle scopes in the crown molding. "You know the rules. I could get in trouble from the Lord's Army, like that."

"Bitch, give me the package!" The agent spat. The courier took a step back and cradled the package to her chest.

"Okay, okay," the agent sighed. "I think I might have a spare wand in my kitchen. Hang on." Storming back into her apartment and slamming the door behind her, she thought about her options. She hadn't been able to find her wand for week. Roger, as much as she found him a saddening figure, was her primary source of income. And he hadn't had a new book in a year. The side projects, yes—but the ghost writers and translators made their cuts larger and larger, the custom freight to Roger's market strongholds— White Vegas, Nebraskan Rhodesia, the Dobsonpods on the Yellow Sea, Pentecosta—were getting more restrictive. And they were strongholds, not strangleholds. Newer, semiliterate thriller authors were rising. Thugs, Roger called them, even some reeducated Asians and Arabs, but they gave people what they wanted. Words garnished with blood. Roger was about ideas, his ideas about the state. With each passing year after Operation Mexico Moon, the agent cared about those ideas less and less. The agent had to eat and pay for the apartment, not to mention the retainer fee for the building's security detail. She thought about what she had to do, walking to her bedroom, and what she had to do made her sad.

She would not tell Roger.

She came back and opened the door, rather amazed that the courier was still standing there. The agent raised her arm and tasered the courier's face. Wasn't a clean shot; the stinger punctured her cheek, straight through. The courier fell back and the agent kicked the package through her apartment door, rubbing the arm brace where her taser was attached. She then unhooked the wire, which would dissolve in about an hour. Kneeling down to the courier she said, "I warned you. It's my risk. It's my package. Why should you give a fuck if I get blown up by it? I have no family left to sue you. And you can fuck your Lord, you fucking hear me?" She stood up and rolled the courier into the freight elevator, and pressed Down.

She decided she needed wine before opening the package. After a half a bottle, Quebecois Concord vintage, she cut open the package with a butcher knife. Black duct tape all along the perimeter, thicker than the packaging itself. Then she extracted the notebook. Thick gray cover, gray wire spirals. The pages were soft, cheap paper, almost decomposing, unlined. Roger's cursive alternated between blue ink and pencil. The agent couldn't make heads or tails of it.

"Fuck," she said to herself, taking the wine from the bottle. "Was he thirteen when he wrote this?" Then she slept, dreaming of elephants in rivers electrocuted by lightning. They were trying to cross to tell the agent something, but she kept saying, turn back, turn back! When she woke, she took the tube out of her ear and shook it.

"Ah," she said, then stared at the notebook. Then Roger called.

"Well?" he said.

"I don't know what to tell you, Roger," she said. "It's really . . . dense." She rubbed her arm where she had attached the taser. "I'm going to have to bring in a consultant."

"Who?" On the other end, she heard his apprentice scrubbing a floor and running a hose. Roger had good grandchildren, who went to good schools. He boarded writers-in-residence each year from his pool of readerly constituents. This year it was only one writer. He would not trust his apprentice with his notebook; she did his chores. The other Minnesotans in his complex, which used to be the Minnesota Zoo, tolerated him because he was famous.

"I'm . . . not sure yet," she said, although she was sure. "Don't worry about it. Listen, what is the novel about? Why don't you pitch it to me?" She laughed, uneasy. It was a long time since Roger had to pitch anything.

"I . . ." Roger stopped and the agent could hear him fumbling for a drink. "That novel was really, really early. I was still working as a bartender, you know? I was still trying to figure out what I needed to do, find my own voice . . . It's like I put everything I didn't want to become in that novel . . ."

"Wait, so it's not a thriller? It's not a Mick Solon book?" Mick Solon was Roger's prime character. Roger wrote series after series of Mick Solon books: Mick assassinating socialist governors, Mick putting newspaper editors on the rack, Mick breaking up Mexican farmers' unions that threatened the state. Above all else, Mick was money.

"Well, not really . . . I mean, it has a character named Mick Solon, but he's not the same . . ."

"Not the same?"

"He's a bit . . . mellower."

"Christ, Roger. What am I supposed to do with this? Will you please tell me what the fuck it's about?"

"It's about relationships," he said. He sounded embarrassed, and a bit surly. "There's a failing marriage. I'm pretty sure there aren't any terrorists in it? But, who the fuck cares. You're my agent.

I want you to fucking assess it and sell it. Maybe I could go over it again, add a political subplot, a liberal suicide bomber? Maybe one of the characters has an affair with a sultan's daughter, who's actually been programmed to kill the Republican senator to make sure tax cuts don't go through, because the taxes are going to fund restoration of the Caliphate?"

"I don't know, Roger. It sounds kind of retro. Stuck in the past?" The Republicans shattered with the Constitution, like all else, like every other party, every other public interest.

"Well, it *is* set in the past. I'm just thinking out loud here. Look, you're my employee."

"Contractor."

"Whatever. Just transcribe the manuscript and figure out what to do with it."

"Fine." She hung up on him. Then she called the front desk. She was going to work harder for this twenty-five percent cut than she ever had in her life.

"Security detail, please. I need to go to Kinko's."

She met the concierge in the front lobby. He was in urban camo and had a silver bag slung over his shoulder like a purse. She didn't want to know what he had in there. He was pretty much a kid. He must have thought she was ancient, and he knew he was trying not to stare at the cloverleaf radiation burn on her cheek.

"All right, ma'am," he said, unholstering his sword and turning its crank to power it up. Ma'am. "Follow me."

They put on their masks. She crossed her arms and followed him out the door. He walked a few paces in front of her in the street. The Kinko's was only two blocks away, but she didn't want to take any chances. She clutched the notebook close to her chest. It was dusk, and the clouds cast shadows over the rowhouses of Queens, in one of the few sustainable neighborhoods left in the old boroughs. Glittering dust swirled around her feet. She almost slipped on the gangplank and a few bicycles nearly ran her over, but the concierge barked at one of the cyclists as he passed and the other that followed got the message. From the Starbucks on the corner of Vine and Polk, a teenage girl watched them pass. The Starbucks window was about a foot thick. She must have been a viceroy's daughter, or a sphere-of-influence envoy, right off the dirigible from China. The agent felt sorry for her, for having to live in this shithole. Lord Manhattan and his revolutionary army could only survive because of the influx of humanitarian aid from Africa and Asia, most of which he kept. And the tourism—plenty of brisk trade to the vaporized sites.

"We're here," the concierge said, moving toward the storefront, looking up at the sky for any security breaches. The gangplank was short by about two feet, so the agent did her best to pick through the mud, coal, and fishbones in front of the Kinko's. Her shoes weren't the best. The concierge gave her a hand. His arm was like a steel beam that she gripped tightly.

"Thank you," she said. He opened the door. She was paying for that courtesy, too.

When she went into the door, she saw that the couriers were waiting for her there, next to the scanners. There was no point in running.

They let her scan the documents and send them to Amar, though. She was surprised about that. But they also said that an equal measure deserved equal measure. The courier she tasered was not there. The concierge thought about protecting the agent, but he was outnumbered five to one, and the couriers had these wiry, muscular bodies. And besides, they were under contract with Lord Manhattan, and he wanted no part with him. He sheathed his sword.

"Stupid," one of the couriers said as he held the agent down next to the paper cutter.

"You can hold her hand if you want," another courier said to the concierge. The agent turned her head toward him, and her feet nearly slipped on the wet straw. She could see that he was contemplating leaving her there and she started screaming and crying.

"What's got into you?" a courier said. "Hold still."

The concierge then took her hand, and she clenched it, dug her nails into him, to the point of almost striking blood. After that, she closed her eyes and she could only hear their voices, and wondered what Roger would think of her.

"Heat it up."

"We can't heat it up. Nothing to do that here . . . none of these machines will do that."

"The bindery? There's a glue-heater on the top—"

"Fuck that. We don't have any pamphlets to bind. I'm not going to pay-n-pedal simply to cauterize an awl."

"Fine. Fine. I don't know if Marigold would really want to cause this one too much harm though."

"She's not the best judge of that now, is she? She was stupid enough to get wounded."

Then they started arguing in Telugu.

Thirty seconds later the awl went through the agent's cheek, through the cloverleaf lesion, to the other side, scraping against her molars. Then she passed out and the concierge let go of her hand.

Amar didn't know any of this. He was at the beach when he received the compressed files. His family was in the water, along with hundreds of other fathers' families. Roger's novel tried to download to Amar's wristwatch, but the memory constrictions were too tight. He had worked with the agent before in the past, regarding Roger's increasingly erratic hand at writing. The agent always thought of Roger's hands shaking when he typed or dictated his novels, but Amar never got that sense. He only saw the information at hand.

He squinted at the file name report on his watch—the sun was bright—looking for clues. The scanners captured words in their filing nomenclature, before downloading the scans in full at Amar's home: BARBARIAN 20-35.ppgr, DEVIL-ROCK.ppgr, LUCY-IS-AT-A-BAR 450?-.ppgr. More unusual gems: Knives . . . a kiss . . . more devils . . . a hill with a cathedral . . .

"Early draft," the agent had punched into the scanner, with fingers she could barely control, her face bandaged like a mummy's. "Please."

Amar's youngest son Prius came running up the beach toward him, from the Bay, waving his arms like wings.

"Watch out for the glass!" Amar shouted, covering his watch with his other hand so that his son wouldn't splash any saltwater on its face, large as a saucer.

"I saw an eel," his son said, as he got closer, panting heavily. "But I escaped it."

"I don't think there are any eels in these waters," Amar said, looking out at the Bay. "And the lifeguards would kill them on sight."

"Oh but there are!" his son said, plopping down on the edge of the towel and pushing his feet into the gravelly sand. Amar winced and turned his body so the watch wouldn't face his son.

"If you say so," he mumbled, giving a smile. Looking at his watch again at a slant, with the file names cascading on the screen, he wondered whether there was a glitch in the transfer. Nothing of the Eighth Client's files had ever looked like this before. The enjoyable voices on the beach kept murmuring over him. Surely there were others like him here?

"You're not working, are you?" his wife said, putting a hand on his shoulder from behind. He flinched.

"You surprised me," he said, looking down.

"You *are* working. Amar . . . you need to take that stupid thing off." She stood over him, blocking the sun, crossing her arms. He met his wife at the Technical Freelance Armory, a few years after Mexico Moon, which in their vendor-conglomerate's handbook was called the Strategic Reorganization of the Americas. She was in marketing services for a Bengali pharmaceutical company. She was shy but was finding her career voice over the last few years after birthing the two children, traveling all over India and Africa to meet her production teams. She was a team leader in a way that Amar could never be. People thought he sounded like a woman on the phone!

"I really need to . . . sorry," he said. "Sorry." He looked toward the Bay, the spires of old Visakhapatnam out in the water. "Where's Puneet?"

"I thought he was getting rasgulla?" His wife looked back at the beach-house, the snack bar, the Ferris wheel.

"No, no—he was with you in the water?"

"I wasn't in the water."

"He's swimming!" his younger son said. "Way out, near the towers."

"Puneet!" his wife shouted, running out to the water. Amar struggled to get his watch off, but the strap was caught on a hook. As he was fumbling, his mind drifted backward, into an undertow of time, and he kept thinking: Why am I panicking? Is it because of her? Why is she panicking?

Back in the van—Amar was actually relieved that the trip to the beach was cut short by an imaginary emergency—Puneet was reluctantly explaining how he was swimming out to the tower crowns to impress a girl. Who wasn't even Buddhist—his wife assumed, thinking out loud, working through the implications, because if this girl was Buddhist, he wouldn't have had need to impress her, on the breakwalls and ruins of the old port, because of their mutual understanding of their dual nonbeing.

Puneet said nothing as they drove farther up into the hills, trees ripe with mango hybrids overhanging the road. Amar didn't dare venture into this emotional territory—he really couldn't care—of course, he was glad his son was safe, but he had no real doubts on this score in the first place. His wife also drifted into silence. But she had larger issues, which soon became clear after Amar glanced at his watch while driving. "I wish you wouldn't work with devils!" she said, looking straight ahead.

"Father works with devils?" his youngest said. "What are they like?"

"They're not devils."

"According to Nichiren they are," his wife said.

Amar sighed and clenched the wheel of the van tighter. They had met at sangha within the technical college, chanting together. The sanghas were subsidized by the companies; after the Japanese diaspora, Nichiren Buddhism had found a home within the corporations of India. He found it as a way to get ahead, but she fell into Nichiren's teachings, more and more every year.

"We're not going to talk about that now," Amar said.

"America is a poisoned land!"

"I've never met them, my beautiful wife," he said between clenched teeth. "They're only contracts I have with them. Now let me drive."

That night, after his children and wife were asleep, he locked himself in his office with the novel. He had managed to survive the sullen hours after they returned from the beach—helping with dinner, chanting together for world peace, doing laundry while his wife helped Prius with his Mandarin homework. Sand was everywhere. Children on motorcycles sped by on their street, which his wife tut-tutted as she was getting ready for bed. Didn't their parents know this was a good Buddhist neighborhood?

"I can't sleep," he said, sitting up after ten minutes.

"Amar, I love you."

"I know." He kissed her forehead. The night sky was still. She was asleep when she said this. She would only say these words with such fierceness and warmth when she was dreaming.

He poured a Scotch—bottle kept in a secret drawer—and started downloading the scans from his watch. He had to enter the writer's world, and this usually wasn't an enjoyable process. It was never clear what an American writer was ever trying to say. Sometimes it made it easier to move the text along, toward a vision or instinct that Amar felt within the words, but sometimes this ambiguity was a dull wall, too thick to break. Tunneling underneath the text to the other side was the only option, but it was long and painstaking. This novel was, as Amar feared, one of the latter cases.

If it could be called a novel. The beginning picked up in the middle of the action, in the middle of a dinner party. In a castle? Amar wondered if, perhaps, the agent had forgotten to send pages, but no—the author had clearly numbered each page of the manuscript with tiny, fastidious numbers and dates, as if the author was trying to assert a timestamp control that was not there in the text itself:

. . . meeting Mick inside the cathedral was not Mary's cup of tea. She was afraid of it, how it loomed on the hill, the votive candles in the vestibule. She had been there before as a child. But Mick said it was the only safe place, where his wife wouldn't discover the true feelings for Mary that he had to keep secret.

"I have to see you," he said. "That, or else I'll leave the city and backpack through Asia. You know, see the world. You may hear back from me or you may not."

"Fine. It's a deal, then," she said.

Mick's wife had learned to read lips when she was in the foreign service. At the kitchen table, she read her husband's conversation as if it were like a book. As Marigold walked up the hill to the cathedral—it was a pleasant path, lit with daffodils—she had no idea that Mick's wife was following twenty paces behind. Mick Solon was already there, lighting a candle and stuffing a dollar in the donation box, supposedly for his dead grandmother.

CHAPTER SIX: Please Don't Kill Me!

This was written more than twenty years ago. This was depressing, all the more depressing after the second Scotch. The handwriting was frantic. The pages had stains—from alcohol, no doubt. Writers like this one always drank. Amar converted the cursive to type, page by page, once he entered his handwriting algorithms. It would take a few hours.

He worked until morning. Decipherment and understanding were two different things, and he was nowhere near understanding when the morning bell rang six times. He could hear his wife wake, shuffle into the kitchen and then the shrine room. He thought about joining her, but would not. One of his project managers from South Africa who always sent him work gave a head's up that a two volume commentary on the Lotus Sutra, by some Zulu pop transhumanist he'd never heard of, was going to be coming his way in a few days, just a head's up.

He was almost falling asleep at his desk, the pages churning with due industry, when his scanner choked and stopped:

"Larissa paused. 'Do you really expect me to discuss politics, my lord?' she said, looking downward. And then her favorite Don Henley song started playing."

White paper on the facing page. The scanner was adjusting to the typography differential. A note was caught in the agent's original scan, pressed in the pages of the notebook. Clean, dark printing, could have been from a typewriter. Creased once in the middle. A logo in the upper center—a seal, to be exact. He recognized that seal. He wished he could have smelled the page.

He blew up the page and read the note, and then read it again more quickly, as if blurring his comprehension would somehow change the placement of the words into something far more innocuous. Then he grabbed the wastebasket underneath his desk and vomited into it. He could hear his wife chanting, and the crossing guard's whistle for school's first shift. His children were second shift but had half-internships that started at nine. They would be waking soon, and his wife would ready them, and Amar started crying.

Then he paused the scanner and called the agent. He wasn't even sure what time it was there, but he didn't care. He waited about a minute for someone to pick up, but it wasn't the agent. The room on the other side was dark, and he could barely see the shapes: a lamp, a head, a gun. Then the head moved closer to the camera.

"Yes, hi?" the woman said. She was young, thin, had a bandaged face. Was chewing something. Kind of evil-looking, Amar thought. She dipped out of view again until she was just a shadow.

"Where's . . . where's the resident of this property?" he said.

"Who are you?" she said.

"I'm a business associate of the woman who lives here. I need to speak to her."

"Oh," she said. "Um . . ." She scratched her hair with both hands. "That's . . . that's really not going to be possible. She's been taken to the Lord."

Marigold wasn't sure what to do with the man on the other side. The agent's apartment was given to her as part of the punishment. They kept adding conditions onto the agent's punishment; Marigold wasn't sure how she felt about that. First the lancing—Marigold was squeamish about it, but fine, it had to be done. People wanted it done. Then the agent was told she was free to go but then Marigold's superior put his mask back on and said, wait, Marigold needs some place to stay to recover, to convalesce, and Marigold wasn't going to make a big deal of it, but the rest of the couriers thought it was only proper. Marigold never really had a place of her own, just a couch in the couriers' warehouse, on Staten Cape. The concierge—who was quite cooperative during the entire justice operation in the Kinko's, all things considered—was beginning to balk at this, Marigold could tell. After all, the building was under his charge, and the couriers—even though they had the official backing of Lord Manhattan, with all the opportunities in the boroughs opened up to them—were beginning to press their luck a little, Marigold thought. But they insisted, and Marigold did need to sleep off all the excitement and the dull pain that was everywhere on her face, so she relented, and arrangements to move to the fifth floor were made. The concierge bit his tongue and gave the security card to Marigold. He also said to let her know if she "needed anything" but she knew what he meant to say was: "I'll have my eyes on you."

But where was the agent to go? That wasn't really thought through by the couriers. The agent was sitting in a corner, staring at the hot glue drip and mix in the funnel of the binding apparatus, and the dragon moths buzzing around the ceiling bulbs, as if it all was happening to someone else. In a way, it was; she didn't seem the type, after what she had been through, to stir up trouble anymore. She wouldn't have been a recurrent threat, Marigold knew that. But the others didn't see it this way.

"She just can't be wandering Queens," one of the couriers said, as if concerned.

"No, no . . ." Marigold's assistant supervisor said. "She'll be safest in the Lord's custody, wouldn't she? For her own protection. Marigold, don't worry. She's going to be all right."

Her assistant supervisor might have noticed a look of concern on Marigold's face as she watched the agent trying to stand up, say something. The agent couldn't get her footing though.

"I think she's going into shock," Marigold said, forcing herself to look at her assistant supervisor, who plucked her from the street, literally, when she was ten, in a neutral-car derby on the old Brooklyn Slags. Marigold was ten, and steered the Acura chassis down the 500 foot incline. The car came in third, even though it crashed into the breakwalls. In the wreckage, her future assistant supervisor had snatched her out and splinted her broken leg. She wasn't really hurt; he didn't know that her brother was the brake operator in the compressed trunk and had died on impact. Marigold had never told him that. She didn't remember much about that day. But the need to protect him from her own awful truths was slipping away from her.

"I know, I know," he said. "She'll have doctors in the detention facility." He snorted. "She'll have better medical benefits than we do." That was the Lord's line. "All right, get her out of here. Hook that gurney up to my cycle. And Marigold, go to her building now and rest."

Marigold nodded. She looked for the concierge, but he was gone. When she got the key from him later, in his little lobby booth, she was going to tell him about the agent being taken to Lord Manhattan (who wasn't even in Manhattan; White Plains, rather), but he gave her a look that said, I already know, and I'm not taking this lightly.

She thought that the phone call might have been the concierge buzzing her—to play a trick on her, maybe?—so it was a genuine surprise to find Amar on the other end. She didn't know that the agent was an agent. Did something with books, of course, but books weren't really up Marigold's alley. There was a five second delay in the transmissions, so after a few minutes of meaningless back-and-forth, during which the agent's predicament was not established to Amar's satisfaction, Marigold asked him:

"Are you from Albany?"

"What?"

Albany was one of the few freestanding cities around the area she could think of, and also the farthest away she'd ever been. To deliver heart medicine. She biked all the way up there and took the river back and lived to tell about both trips.

"You have a nice office," Marigold said. "And you sound far away. So I was thinking you were maybe from Albany."

Amar licked his lips and closed his eyes. He was sweating. He said, with his eyes still closed: "Could you tell me when she's coming back?" When he opened them, he wanted the agent to be there, to have willed the agent into existence in that room, speaking to him.

Marigold was still there. "Well, that's kind of hard to say," she said. "It depends on how long they treat her."

Amar took a lot longer to speak than the normal delay. "Please tell me she's not hurt."

"Well, a little. But she'll really be all right." She wasn't sure if she sounded convincing.

"Okay . . ." He took a deep breath. "What about the notebook? You have to have the notebook there, right?"

"I . . . Wait, well, was that . . ." She didn't know why she was trying to be so helpful. Maybe she wanted to see his office a little longer—the mahogany desk, the office supply dispenser, the window overlooking what she thought was Albany. But of course it wasn't Albany—the trees and grass, even in Albany, would not have been that green, and the wind shaking those trees would not have been so clear (without specks), and the children's bicycles on the curb would not have been so unstolen.

"You have to tell me!" he said.

"Well, she was going to the Kinko's to scan something—"

Amar leaned back in his chair and sighed, relieved. "Yes, that is the document." For the first time he gave the impression that they were speaking the same language. "Yes, thank you. So where is it?"

"I'm not sure." Marigold knew, however, that her supervisor had discarded it. Maybe that was part of the agent's punishment as well.

A woman entered the office. She was in a dark suit and wore sunglasses with whirling blue lights on the sides. "Amar, is everything all right?"

He turned around and waved both of his hands. "Not now—get out!"

"I heard you screaming, the children—"

"Out!" He stood up from his chair. "Out!"

She saw the wastebasket, the vomit. "Are you sick, Amar?"

"Please . . . please . . ." He opened the door wider and pushed her backward. It took her a few seconds to realize what was happening—Amar never did things like that—but by that time he had shut and locked the door.

"You have a really beautiful wife, Amar."

He squinted. "How do you know my name?"

"She said it. Plus it's on the bottom of the screen. Listen, do you mind if I pee?"

He leaned forward. "Fine. But believe me, I'm not going anywhere. The notebook is—"

She ran to the bathroom, locked the door (not sure why) and sat down on the toilet, and tried to think of what to do next. Amar was too far away to hurt her—she was pretty sure of that—but all the same she didn't want to get other couriers in trouble. If he knew the agent, maybe he knew others in Queens? She was stupid to think that he came from Albany—her mouth couldn't be trusted.

Think, she said to herself, looking at herself in the mirror. Think before you say anything. Think.

When she sat down again, she saw that Amar was staring straight at her. Wouldn't break his eyes away.

"They threw the notebook away," she said.

He didn't get angry; not in a way that was immediately visible to her. He was resigned. "Can I tell you what was in the notebook?"

"Sure," she said.

He laughed. "No, no. You know, I thought about telling you, but . . ."

"Fuck off!" she said, nearly shoving the screen off the desk, kicking it. "You need to leave."

"No, wait. Wait! Listen, the author might call—"

Marigold turned off the feed. Then she left the apartment to do her routes, pushed herself to, even though she wasn't feeling well, or herself. She ran through checkpoints in silence. All the other couriers put their funds together and bought her kicks with a passport transmitter. They were red. She tried to keep herself from crying when she delivered her packages. They were so hand-held: toys, spices, books. She could mule them all, borrow a bicycle through straight-aways when cleared for it, sprint otherwise, jump over barricades, slide feet first under glass-enclosed garden overhangs arching over the streets—"fuck you gardens" the other couriers called them, on account of the old money that made such projects possible on a thoroughfare—the armed gardeners shaking pruning fists once the trespass was discovered. Too late, always too late. She was the rabbit who could slip through any fence. The exhaustion didn't slam her until she bounded up the steps to the agent's apartment, as the day was ending. The agent had nothing but wine to drink, not even safe water.

"Whew," Marigold said, catapulting onto the bed with a non-alcoholic bottle. She checked the messages; one from an R someone. Had to have been the author. She turned on the screen and flinched at the first sight of him. White hair like ash. A face that could have been a training surgeon's palette—too much flesh in one cheek and not enough in the other (both were rosy), a thick nose broken and reset, though not perfectly, a jaw that had molar outlines under the skin like the baby corn cobs she liked to eat from the Chinese charity meal packets. His face was too much for Marigold. She did, upon seeing him, want to know what was in the notebook, but she wanted to hear it from Amar, not this man.

"Hi," the author said. He coughed. Marigold crossed her legs and drank half the bottle while the author gathered his thoughts in the darkness around him. "Hey. Um, listen—I hope you're doing well, by the way—I needed to check in, about your . . . your appraisal of the manuscript. I know, I know, these things take time. You're always telling me to be patient. But I'm . . . I'm really under the gun here." He laughed and took a sip from a red straw. "Grandkids need to eat, to go to school, you know . . . you know?" It was storming in Minnesota. Purple lightning. The gutter purifiers were gathering water off the roof, distilling it through pipes and into basement barrels. He lived in the savannah in the old zoo. Foundations of most of the old buildings existed, but only those. "See, here's the thing. They're raising my levies and fees here. I think it's a plot to get rid of me. I want to write for people in Nebraska, but I don't want to live there, you know?" He sucked the last liquid through the straw. "So I need your assessment . . . soon. Or I'll find another agent." He thought that this last threat would get her attention. "Oh! There is another small issue. There's a piece of memorabilia that happened to be in that notebook. Nothing of too much consequence . . . but, if you could . . . if you could return it to me, it would be much appreciated. You can take the postage out of the future earnings of the book." He rattled his head, to draw him back to the most important matter at hand. "I want a fast sell!" He then hung up and folded up his empty drink box.

A giant sloth brayed outside his window. Only gentle animals lived in the complex anymore, but he still didn't trust them. Then he heard the monorail approaching, creaking through the rain. He sighed and went out to his front porch, and watched the monorail come in.

Inside the front car was that sloth, large as a horse, pawing at the windows. The monorail was automated. Someone from another part of the complex must have lured the sloth onto the monorail and sent it his way. The monorail halted. Could it have been the super? (The super liked to call himself the zookeeper. But he was really just an asshole.)

"Lion savannah," the monorail's calming voice said. "Please exit carefully." The doors to the car, which should have been welded shut with rust years ago, creaked open, and the sloth exited onto the platform in front of Roger's house. The platform was narrow, but the sloth had sure feet, and bobbing its head, moved closer to Roger's front door. Its eyes were yellow and shot.

Below him, the waves of rain rustled the sedge. Swampy run-off. He didn't like venturing down there in the best of conditions, or travel far on foot. Green Path to the theater, Red Path to the general store, Purple Path to the megafauna barn. No. He took the monorail for Friday night cinema. The other tenants liked what they showed on the giant screen more than he did. They were the type of people who enjoyed movies from Bangladesh that didn't make sense—lots of violence, but in the wrong ways and places (Mughal romantic comedies that somehow ended in bloodbaths; a series of six galling musicals following the Ural Mujahideen). Roger only allowed his writers-in-residence to visit the cinema once a month. He didn't want their minds poisoned any more than necessary. Other years he had four, five writers from his readerly provinces learn from him. Numbers dwindled, though. He wasn't sure the sole young woman given to him was up for the job. The monorail closed its doors and creaked forward to the primate house. Roger took a step back and clanged the bell next to his front door. He didn't stop until his apprentice arrived. The sloth was taking its time. The apprentice was taller than he was, and the tan uniform was too short in the sleeves for her. She was out of breath and she smelled like woodsmoke. The walkway from the monorail platform to Roger's raised porch was about twenty feet and had flimsy railings on each side. The house itself was on concrete pillars above the veldt. There was nowhere for the sloth to go except forward and it did. But it was groggy. The sloth had to have been tranquilized.

As it moved closer, Roger could see that something glowing was attached to the fur on its side.

"Apprentice, see what's on its fur."

"What? No."

"Do not disobey a direct order!"

She sighed.

"Did you bring your sidearm?" he said.

She shook her head. "I . . . I was fixing the furnace, like you told me to."

"It's moments like these that provide you the writing material that will change your life forever!" he barked. "And to fully seize the moment, you need to be properly armed. That's the bedrock of this household, do you understand?"

She slowly nodded.

He put a hand on her shoulder, and tried to meet her in the eye, though she would not meet him in the eye. "Fetch your sidearm, and also the rocket launcher from my study."

"Which one?" she asked.

He paused, not wanting to seem too greedy for carnage in front of her. "The small one."

While she was in the house, the sloth did an ambling circle toward him, then shuffled sideways. He darted forward, thinking to himself how brave and stupid he was. But he also wanted to prove to his apprentice that he would not make her do what he would not do himself.

The sloth reeked like shit, and underneath the fur Roger could see sores. Reconstituted, it was not made for these times. He could also see that some bastard had tagged the sloth's hide with iridescent paint. It was a message:

BIG MURDERER

FUCK OFF N DIE

LEAVE

"I've got the weapons," the apprentice said, the pistol in her holster and the rocket launcher slung over her shoulder. "I also brought a notebook and pen . . ." She managed to smile. "In case the inspiration—"

"Give me that," he said, taking the rocket launcher from her, turning off the safety settings. His first thought, which immediately shamed him, was to kill her, to point the rocket launcher ten feet from her chest and to blow a hole through her and send the rest of her into the old lion sanctuary below. His hands shook; he had trouble keeping the rocket launcher level as he arced it past her body—a clear safety violation, how could he be teaching her anything—and toward the sloth. The storm was tapering, though the wind pushed the rain back and forth through the air.

"This is just another example of how the world hates us and our ideas," he said. "You have to keep being strong . . . persisting . . ."

"What's on the fur?" she said. His outbursts and directives were not reaching her. She was getting numb; too numb for his training to have proper effects. She was broken down, but he honestly didn't know whether he had the strength to build her up again. "Do you want me to—"

"It's nothing," he said. "It's one of those Shiite gang symbols."

"That's not nothing," she said.

The sloth raised its head, took a few dizzy steps, and lumbered toward them.

"Kill it!" she shouted at Roger.

He tried to steady himself, lowered his center of gravity. The sloth's tongue sloshed gray. It was a herbivore, but didn't they mix in leopard DNA? Did the zookeeper tell him that once? His feet slipped, and as he fell forward his finger pushed forward on the trigger. The shot screamed, a wall of fire and metal vapor rushed toward him.

He woke up in the middle of the night, on his bed, with the fireplace blazing. The apprentice stood over him.

"You broke your arm," she said. "I splinted it."

"The sloth . . ." he said.

"The rocket smashed into the walkway," she said. Her voice was flat. "The walkway collapsed and the sloth went down. Don't worry. I set up a rope bridge across."

"That can't be safe . . ."

"It's safe enough. I worked the whole day on it."

He tried to sit up. "I need to call the complex security . . . whoever did this . . ."

She gently pushed him down on his good shoulder. "Don't worry. I've already taken care of it. You shouldn't have to tolerate that kind of attack." She took out her notebook, flipping through the corners, and handed him her notebook. "I've written all about it. I free-wrote all night."

He took it from her. He wanted to say he was proud of her.

"But you shouldn't read it until you're feeling better," she said. "I don't know what's going to happen to us, Roger."

"What . . ." He didn't have the strength. He smelled napalm and ash still. He had assumed it was from her earlier chores.

"I learned explosives pretty well from my father. He used to take down Omaha rail lines in the wars. Did you know that you have bags and bags of potash in the basement?"

When she left the bedroom, to set up a defensive perimeter, he read her exercise book.

"THIRD PERSON EXERCISE: MOMENT OF PLOT RESO-LUTION

"*Charity McClune knew who had come to kill them: Dumbocrats, in league with homosexual imams and ecoterrorist Jews, with Mexican footsoldiers brought in from their misguided revolutions, financed by turban-wearing geothermal vice lords from India. They would stop at nothing. She had to stop them. How fitting that the seeds of their own destruction would be carried on a monorail—the transportation of choice for Communists and their broken dreams. She smirked as she assessed her handiwork. She had blonde hair and blue eyes, blue like the glacier waters of her hometown in Free Alaska. She knew the price of freedom and was willing to pay any price for it. Those other people, they were full of hate for her and her teacher, a great American—*"

He flipped forward, hands barely under control.

"*Only one right path lies before her. In the pure fire of justice her world would be cleansed. Looking up, she almost saw in a cloudface her father's face, smiling down on her. She missed him so much and the wind pressed up a gentle breeze on her face as her chief colonel nodded.*

"'*Bring down the noise, Charity!' he exclaimed, his jaw set.*

"*As she clenched the trigger—*"

Roger closed the notebook. "Total shit," he said, falling asleep, drifting backward to the air force bases of his prime, when he was a prime mover, an advisor, a prophet of policy. No one would ever understand, not even the apprentice. The only ones who understood were long dead, at one time laid to rest in desecrated Arlington graves: the rear admirals who requested signed copies of *Fierce Power* by the boxload for mandatory frigate book clubs, the Secretary of Information and Coercion who sent his daughter to shadow him for a week for a school project, and of course the president, the commander-in-chief, *his* commander-in-chief. Roger imagined that others in the inner circle of Washington, Lincoln, and Reagan must have felt the same thrill—not only to be living at the same time as an architect of history, but to advise great men and great decisions, by sheer accident more than anything else. He was, after all, a writer of stories, an entertainer, and he never let himself forget that. And yet . . . he was there when the world changed. He was there. He was there in the bunker, a mile underneath Minot. El Paso burning, Dallas burning, the District of Columbia cordoned, Chinese peacekeepers amassing on the Canadian border, and the choice resting on heavy shoulders.

"Tell me what to do," the president asked him in the bunker's lounge, velvet upholstery muffling any sound, any Klaxons and shouts. The words and the president's face echoed in the chambers of his sleep. "Tell me what to do, Roger."

"Your advisors, sir . . ." Roger said, swirling his bourbon and looking down into it.

"I don't trust them. Don't trust any of them. You know that, Roger." The president could get petulant without enough sleep, but who wouldn't?

"I do know that, sir. I would . . ." Roger set his bourbon down on a stack of his own paperbacks on the coffee table. A poster of Roger on the door stared back at Roger—arms crossed, wearing sunglasses, an ammo belt draped over his shoulders like a scarf, a baseball cap that had embroidered on it: DON'T TREAD ON ME, and underneath that: KILL ZONE. Roger tried to think of what that Roger would do, what Mick Solon would do.

"You have to root out the problem at its source, sir." The commander-in-chief stared at Roger. "Do you understand what I mean, sir?"

The president thought about this, licking his lips. "Do you mean to bomb Mexico City? Nuclearly?"

Roger shrugged and tried to keep his eyes on the president. When the president didn't say anything, Roger said, "Have you seen the war games for that, sir? With the bunker busters?" Roger had no idea whether war games for that even existed, or what his real advisors would say.

"No . . . no. But maybe that's for the better." The president stood up and Roger followed suit. The president reached out to shake his hand and Roger moved right away to salute, leaving the president's hand dangling there. But then the president returned the salute.

"Stay here as long as you want," the president said before leaving, and in two hours the bombers were in the air, reaching their cruising altitude. And Roger did stay in the bunker, for five months, as winter set in, and then—instead of spring—winter set in again throughout the Americas. Then after that, another winter of fog and ash, and the president's hanging at Mount Vernon. Then the third winter skipped right to autumn, winds of acid and ice, the fall of two to three provisional governments, and then no governments at all, at least in the old sense of the word. Roger took a Humvee from Minot to Minneapolis, and he had to pay for the trip with his collection of Liberty dollar coins. The soldiers never talked with him, joshed with him, as they did before. The zoo was the safest place he could find.

Of course, the world stabilized, after a fashion, and he was able to write again. People were still hungry for his stories. They were the same people as before, for the most part, the same survivors. And their children, who had little in the way of television, grew up with Mick Solon instead. Roger found an agent who understood this—his old agent having disappeared in the Manhattan reorganizations. Enclaves still believed in the rightness of Mick's causes, that Mexico Moon was necessary and cleansing, only one salvo in the war for civilization.

Roger obliged them.

When he woke from his long sleep, he was put under house arrest. Not in so many words; no one announced this to him. But there was always an armed groundskeeper within eyesight of his house. The apprentice disappeared, and was found a few days later on the outskirts of the old zoo, where she had set up a makeshift bomb making factory and blew herself up by accident. The apprentice's family demanded that Roger pay for her funeral. He used the request for a fire-starter. There was no body, he wanted to tell them. How can you bury a person without a body? Do you want to bury her jaw? Her femur? Her dental records? The investigation into the destruction of the sloth and the walkway found him neither guilty nor innocent, but rather complicit in a long-standing pattern of harboring and brainwashing terrorists. No charges came, though. On the other hand, they did arrest the fucker who drugged the giant sloth—tampering with megafauna was a serious crime. She was one of the medical assistants, who administered chemo at the free clinic and hated everything Roger stood for. He tried to follow her trial on the daily bulletins, but the painkillers he took for his legs would not let him focus on anything for too long, except for sleep. He tried to call his agent, but couldn't remember the right access codes, and the screen would always stay blank, no matter what he did. Then in the middle of the night he heard the apprentice calling for him, pausing with her blowtorch and asking: Isn't this what you would want me to do? And he would have said, No, not exactly—see, action has to be clean like writing is clean, there have to be clear consequences and no loose ends. Self-defense has to be guided by the conscience of liberty. The fight has to be a true one. People just want to forget about their problems. Also, you're really fucking scaring me.

And she might have paused, after listening to that impromptu lesson, letting it sink in.

But she always went back to her welding.

After a few weeks of this toss-and-turn, he received a package. The sky was clear and inviting when the courier knocked on his door and asked him to sign. The courier was young, barely out of UPS U. It was the first time Roger had gone outside, even a few steps, since the apprentice died.

"What if this is a bomb?" Roger asked.

"I've scanned it," the courier said, waving his black wand. A little too casual for Roger's taste. "It's fine."

Roger pulled the package to him and closed the door. The box was taped over and over again. He set it on the kitchen table and then saw it had a passport from India.

"Shit!" Roger said, swiping at the package and pushing it to the floor. Maybe there was a contact poison. Those stupid wands couldn't account for everything. He let the package sit there for a few more days, until he summed up the courage to face his own death. Placing the package back on the table, he closed his eyes as he cut it open with scissors and reached inside. It was a manuscript. His manuscript, a copy of it, scribbled upon in red ink. In his haze he had forgotten about it. There was a handwritten letter attached to it.

Dear Sir:
You may be surprised to find this returned to you, as you have not had any dealings with me in the past. However, your agent—who I now fear to be dead—has often utilized my services to doctor your recent synopses and novels, though I am rarely able to make sense of them. It took me great trouble to track you down. I assume you are in hiding.

I have enclosed my transcription and my edits, in order to complete my contract and rid myself of you. I have to say that I found the ideas devoid of meaning, the characters cold, the prose poorly written—like everything else of yours. And yet, in a manner utterly alien to your later projects, there is a vulnerability too. The people that inhabit these pages are shallow but they are not inhuman. You started with something at least honest—in your own fashion—and cast that aside.

You had a letter stuck in the pages of your notebook. Do you remember this letter? You must. It's a letter of commendation from the last president of the United States, "personally, and with great warmth, thanking you for defending the Constitution and the integrity of the nation during a time of great trial."

The letter goes on to list the names of the bomber pilots who "would vouch for the great effect your writing had on their thoughts as they dropped the collateral payload on the enemies of America and freedom." These words made me—

Amar felt his wife's hands on his shoulders in the middle of his composition. He flinched, though he didn't want to.

"Let it go for now," she said. "The children are asleep." She curled closer into him, arms around his neck. He felt that she was naked. A torrent had come into her when he told her everything, about every distant monster he had to face, the innocent blood embedded in every file. The planes taking off, and landing lighter six hours later.

She told him that even monsters needed to be forgiven—not right away, of course. But even Devadatta, the Buddha's worst enemy, the traitor of his inner circle, was able to be a great enlightened teacher after many successive lives, after many hells and trials. She had told him that calamity was the loom and that all sentient beings were the cords of silk on the loom, interwoven in the warp and the woof, bound tightly together. She struggled to find the spirit of these words, but even this attempt comforted him. It gave him the courage to write the letter to the American—which his wife needed to interrupt. She told him she needed him. He turned around his chair and kissed her neck, then licked each nipple as she pushed herself onto him. She unclasped his pants and slid his cock out, rubbing its head and pressing it against the tangle of her pubic hair. He put his hands on her ass and guided himself into her.

She came first. After he came, she lifted herself off and knelt in front of him. She sucked his softening cock and ran her tongue on the foreskin until it was clean, and then placed her head against his thigh. He stroked her hair and told her he was ready to finish the letter. He wanted to finish strong, vicious, to devastate the author so that he would never be able to write another word again. And then Amar could go on with his life.

After she left, he sat there for a long while. No words came to him. He had no idea what to say next. That girl who thought he lived in Albany—what would she have told him? She would have told Amar (or so he imagined) that he didn't have the right to say anything, really, even to a war criminal, that he was trying to dredge up memories he didn't possess of a time he didn't live through. And that it was better to quit while he was ahead and pretend none of those false memories ever existed.

Really, she would be all right.

The wound on her cheek—he closed his eyes and saw her lean forward—look, Amar, it's healing.

Plight of the Sycophant

The border between the two worlds is hard to describe but easy to feel under the skin. Even a few miles away, you can sense its effect, in ways that you'll probably never understand. Much like when a person puts a gun in your mouth (though this has never happened to me). The bullet doesn't leave the gun—anticipation is its own weapon. And fear. One must never forget fear.

You can have this unsettling feeling on either side of the border, though you will likely prefer one side to the other. One world to the other. The sun will be bright, as it always is in this part of the world—except, perhaps, for September—and the giant angels will be patrolling the mist, as they always do. There will often be rainbows, on account of this bright sun and the mist. They grow boring.

The border is not actually a wall but a waterfall. No one knows where the water comes from; there is never a cloud in the sky. But the water comes. The angels are rather mean and swear a lot. They wear bright, yellow ponchos, with a red script in their language up and down the sleeves. There is only one checkpoint, one place to cross by foot (although it is not advised) or car. The cars have to be coated in a certain type of myrrh, or else the border patrol would not even consider letting you cross. And even then you have to have the right kinds of papers, the right bribes. And—the hardest part—the right attitude. Angels will detain a person trying to cross for months, sometimes years, trying to find out what attitude a border-crosser might have. What desires they have. Their prisons near the gate are little cottages and are actually kind of cute.

Sometimes the angels are satisfied by the answers and sometimes they are not. Some travelers end up leaving their cottages, and some do not.

This is all, of course, from my perspective, from my country. I have never been to the other country. I have not had appropriate business to take me there. And I'm afraid of the angels. They're not actual angels. That I'll grant you. They don't fly, or sing, or help people. But they are certainly tall—seven feet, maybe eight feet in height. They don't have wings, but their guns do. I've seen one of their guns fly, once. I was emptying the grease trap from the store—surely the nastiest job in the history of the world; believe me, there's a lot of competition—out in the garbage pit closer to the waterfall. One of the angels had to re-strap his boot and the gun flapped furiously to stay aloft, like a hummingbird, and it did. The wings fluttered in a manner that my eye couldn't catch. I was watching it all with binoculars; the pit wasn't *that* close to the waterfall, and anyway, I didn't have a garbage permit, so I had to watch out for patrols. Fees and levies were designed to keep us safe—but if I actually *paid* them, then we'd be operating at a loss. Plus the scavengers around the pit liked the grease, and they were bold night and day—green bears and millipedes large as my arm. I was already risking an arm and a leg.

Anyway, the pawn shop where I work is in sight of the border. It's the last chance for a traveler to get rid of his or her belongings before going over to the other side—or maybe pick up something that might be useful farther down the road. We also sell fuel. By popular demand. And also hot dogs, frozen goods, pop, batteries, and the like. But we're not a convenience store. We sell a lot of beer and guns. Not the angel's guns, but regular guns. They're not allowed across the border, so people get what they can for them. There's always something going on in the shop—a lot of tourists come through, just to get a *look* at the waterfall, but you still get bored at the register. A pawn shop is a pawn shop.

No one comes back from the other side. In case you're wondering.

And just where does the water go, once it has fallen? You'd think that the ground would flood, but it doesn't. There might be grates leading into a sewer system, or something. There might be a vast, underground ocean under the surface of the earth, where merpeople live ordinary, screwed up lives in screwed up mer-civilizations, and no one can figure out where that waterfall comes from. I couldn't say one way or another, and there's no chance I'll find out.

There was only one time, years ago, when I came awfully close. Or at least, I thought I did; now I'm not so sure. I'm not sure what side I come down on. It was the time I was a sycophant, and it wasn't pretty. I was twenty, or thereabouts, young and stupid, and I'd only been at the pawn shop for a year. I had wandered for a while before that, and since I couldn't find a way past the border, I stopped and looked for a job. No one liked to pump gas and pawn guns in sight of the angels, so the station was always hiring. Turnover is hell. But I kept my nose clean. I had a trailer that I was actually proud of. No one lived around me. I had no idea how lonely I was, especially after my double shifts.

It was at the tail end of one of those double shifts when a woman came in to tell me her car broke down, and could she get some help. It was Sunday, going on evening, and no one credible in town was going to jump-start her car, or fix her flat. Which was where I came in. She had her hair in a beehive bun, and wore a T-shirt that looked wooly and too warm. I figured she was driving from a ways off; she had a funny accent. I asked her where her car was. About three miles that way, she said. She pointed north, parallel to the border. My brother's still in the car. He's guarding it.

Like an angel? I said.

I . . . I guess, she said. It was even more obvious she wasn't from around here.

I smelled her then—acrid, sour raspberries. It didn't smell like the stench of a long road trip, but neither did it smell like perfume.

But I was bored all the time, like I said before, and so the intrigue won out against my better judgment. She was something different. I decided that I could be some use to her, and the blood in my head pounded.

Okay, I said. I'll help you in 15 minutes. Can you wait 15 minutes? That's when I get off.

She thanked me, and she seemed sincere, and she smiled. I became aroused. She was perfectly pretty, and I wasn't ashamed to notice this. It was a reaction—I knew that I wouldn't *act* on the reaction ever. It just wasn't how I operated, to make huge, unyielding assumptions about what a smile meant.

After my replacement came—I forget his name, after all of these years, like I've forgotten a lot of things—I took her to my car. A filthy Civic. It was embarrassing, but she didn't seem to mind the birdcages and miniature sinball games strewn on the floor of the shotgun seat. I also had a gun behind my shotgun seat—just a pistol, a non-angelic gun. The birdcages were from a man who pawned about a dozen parakeets on us. I'd bought them and set them free. I felt pretty bad for them, and no one was going to buy them.

Oh, just move that stuff out of the way, I said, starting the car. I was more ashamed about my vehicle than my erection. The erection was a private matter, while the car was definitely public space.

She smiled, not to me really, and rolled down the window. She was serene, undisturbed.

I love the breeze, she said, sticking her arm out as I pulled out. The mist, too.

The mist is pretty nice, I said. I hadn't gotten bored of the mist yet. It was fine and soft enough that you would realize, with the right wind, that your face was wet and cool. The mist made the heat bearable.

I drove closer to the waterfall. The land was a wasteland: no hills, no vegetation, all dust and sand and sandstone. After about a minute, she said: turn down that road there.

I tried and tried but couldn't place her accent at all. I usually had an ear for those kinds of things. My father, right as I left his house to seek my fortune, told me that I would always be wandering around the bottom of the world. Actually he shouted it as I was walking away. I think he had meant it as a curse, but I never saw him again anyway. I didn't want to ask her about the accent, where she came from.

But I wondered if I would find out anyway. I'd stupidly hoped that she'd abandon her brother and come with me back to my trailer for a few whiskey sours and she'd clench herself against me on my sofa (brand: "Sof-ahh . . ."), and I'd say, no, the sofa folds out, it's a hide-a-bed. Or something along those lines. This was breaking my vow of nonintervention that I made when I met her. I know that. But I didn't know what to expect. I figured there was a chance she wanted me, and that I could help her along the process of wanting me. I was, however, afraid of my own mouth, the bombshells that would pirouette from it.

Her arm hanging out the window did a little dance, a little hand puppetry, and she closed her eyes.

After she closed her eyes, I put away my seduction plan, folded it up like a map. It was a dumb plan anyway.

The road running parallel to the border was a kind of service alley at first, filled with speed bumps, behind fast food restaurants and hotels you'd pay for by the hour. "Hotel" was probably too kind of a word. But then the sprawl stopped and the road turned dirt. Soon we were in the bona fide desert, and the border was a half-mile east of us. I heard the waterfall roar and, peering into the mist, saw the silhouettes of angels—or at least their bright ponchos—here and there.

I hadn't known about this road at all. (It has since disappeared altogether. The main road fades into pure desert now. The beginning of the service alley that I remember is now an abandoned waterpark. Once a year I go looking for the road she took, but no luck.) It was bumpy, and the Civic's shocks were horrible. I apologized about the smoothness, or the lack of it, of the ride.

She must have been sleeping, or meditating, or something. She opened her eyes. What did you say?

The road is bumpy, I managed.

She shrugged. I told you I had a brother, right?

I think so, I said. A sudden spray turned the windshield to a fine mud and I turned on the wipers.

He has a birth defect, she said. I think I failed to mention this. Just to warn you, so you don't become alarmed or anything.

I nodded and smiled, as if to say, no problem, whatever. I was secretly troubled. I wished that the brother wasn't in the picture at all, that I could take care of her car trouble with no familial witnesses. Perhaps, I reasoned, like I imagined a snake would reason, his birth defect meant that he was only a shell of a person, and could not interfere in any relationship that might develop between me and the stranded woman.

The sun was beginning to set. We hit a pothole and, startled, she grabbed my hand. Hers was warm but mine was warmer. She pulled away and didn't meet my gaze, even though I was offering it to her.

At last we reached her car, which was actually a Hummer. Maybe they were drug dealers, I thought, or smugglers, although that would have been impossible, on account of the waterfall border and the angels. I pulled up next to the Hummer and we got out.

Thank you *so much*, she said, sounding like she really meant it. She stretched her arms up.

No problem, I said. Happy to help. Let me look at the engine. Can you pop the hood?

I glanced at the interior of the car, looking for her brother. The windows of the Hummer didn't have tinting, and I could see her brother lying across one of the backseats. I forget which backseat, as there were three in the SUV. He seemed to be made out of water. He wore dark glasses that didn't seem to be made of water, but that was it. Water. I could see right through his body. He looked a few years younger than she was. But for crying out loud—gauging such a thing was totally without value. Talk about a birth defect. I wasn't scared of him though.

She didn't pop the hood, like I'd asked. She just kept stretching. At first her arms, and then her legs, as if she was getting ready to sprint. I almost wanted to cry. Instead I said: Is this some kind of joke? A prank? Is your car perfectly fine or is it not?

She then told me that I was to drive the Hummer into the waterfall.

But I'd die, I said. You'd die, too. If the angels don't kill you— and they will—well, you can't get through the waterfall. It can't be penetrated. It just can't.

She then explained to me how she wouldn't die, because she wouldn't be in the Hummer. She would just be watching, watching out for angels who might start to get ideas and try to stop them. And then she would stop *them*.

Even though she didn't threaten me, per se, I guess I should have been a little afraid of her threat-like statements.

But instead I laughed. I was getting angry, that she only had wanted to use me. Not to fix a car, which was perfectly legitimate. But rather to drive, in suicidal fashion, in reach of the angels. I had worked myself into a lather over this? I wanted to please her, but not at such a steep, ridiculous price.

Stop angels, I said. Huh.

Absolutely, she said. She stopped her stretching and walked toward me. Do you know what's on the other side? Do you know what's in the other country?

No, what, I said. Try me.

I was ready, at that point, to drive away, good riddance.

People like me, she said.

She then revealed her true face, which I really don't want to talk about any more than I absolutely have to.

At any rate, after her revelation, I saw her point rather clearly, and I asked what I could do to help. Anything to help. I was desperate to, and there wasn't really any question about any previous, skeptical thought processes that I might have had regarding her and her needs.

She hid her true face again—one glance was enough for me to become her sycophant, no need to overdo it—and then explained the rest of her plan, which I considered extremely cunning.

My brother is the safecracker, she said, in her honeyed voice. He can turn off the waterfall, at least for a few instants. Your purpose—and it is a very noble purpose—is to collide into the waterfall and kill yourself. There's a good chance there'll be a spectacular explosion, which would be a nice touch. This will distract the angels just long enough for my brother and I to pass through.

Got it, I said. And so you'll be in the mist near the car, waiting for your brother to open up the waterfall.

Exactly! I knew you'd understand.

I was pleased by her words. I wanted to befriend her, now even more so, and this seemed to be the only way. I wished, naturally, that I wouldn't have to die to curry her favor. Barring mental disorder, or some kind of severe, unbearable depression, who wouldn't? But I searched the catacombs of my brain over and over, and came across only dead ends where any objections should have been. So that decided things.

Okay, I said, I'm ready! Let's do this.

She threw me the keys. The wind blew her wooly shirt up a little. I could see for a second some kind of armor above her knees. At this point my desire for her wasn't sexual at all. It was pure and altruistic. This point should be clear.

Okay, she said. Why don't you drive a little closer. Into the mist. I'll walk alongside the car, so drive slowly.

Great! I said. I'd never been happier. I opened the car door, stepped inside, and started the Hummer up. I began to buckle my seat belt, but that seemed absurd, considering that the *point* was to kill myself. Safety wasn't coming first. Her brother—although I wasn't sure whether it was her brother at all—was still laying behind me, totally still. He didn't say anything, but then I saw he had an orange handkerchief covering his mouth. It was almost like the handkerchief was gagging him.

Hey, I said behind me, taking the Hummer out of park and letting it crawl forward, on Lydia's signal. I knew her name was Lydia all of the sudden. I didn't know the water-guy's name; otherwise I would have used it.

He still didn't say anything. I wondered briefly if the handkerchief in his mouth was impeding his speech. But I was preoccupied with the driving, really.

You'll be able to do your thing soon enough, I told him. And then you'll be home free. Scotch free.

The man tried to say something, but it was muffled.

Did you say anything? Lydia asked me.

The man's eyes widened and he shook his head. I didn't know why it was important to him, but I called out to her: No, you must be hearing things.

I loved her! But the guy relaxed. He must have loved her, too, and wanted to please her; otherwise, he wouldn't be in this position.

I want to say, at this point, that in no way did I believe I was a sycophant. I was merely doing what I thought was in my best interest, which happened to be in her best interest. Others might consider alignment of desire some kind of flattery. But it's not the same. Even now, I'm not sure what to think about that time in the desert with Lydia and her brother. I had a customer come in about a week ago who was an angel. I didn't think this was at all strange. Why was that? He wanted chaw and ethanol for his truck, but he didn't seem to have a truck. He did, however, have a sword strapped to his belt. He wasn't wearing his poncho and seemed even taller up close. And there was no winged gun in sight. The sign on my door said BANS GUNNED ON PREMISES, but the sign didn't say anything about edged weapons. And what was a PREMISES, anyway? A group of more than one premise? Every word, in the presence of the angel, seemed to be utterly beautiful and yet completely falter as a means to communicate. He blinked at me, and he paid for the chaw, and I told him that we didn't have any ethanol-substitute fuel, we weren't really positioned in a progressive part of the country. He appeared mildly upset. It's for my truck, it's broken down just outside of town, he said. I pretended he wasn't there. Finally, he gave up on me. Have a good day! I called out to him as he left. Then I noticed that there was moss in the ice cream sandwiches case, and that I should probably clean it out after I closed.

To call the moment dreamlike would have been inaccurate. My life was normal and real—and yet I did things for reasons I didn't understand, all the time. Especially when I was younger.

None of this was on my mind in the desert with Lydia, though.

After a minute she tapped my window and I stopped. The mist from the waterfall was really bad for driving, or good for hiding, depending on how you looked at it. I turned on the windshield wipers, because I wanted to see as clearly as possible when I slammed into the waterfall and killed myself.

Look there, she said, pointing to the eastern edge of the border, in the direction of the checkpoint.

I don't see anything, I said. I wished I had had my binoculars—for no other reason than to give them to Lydia.

An angel is walking toward us, she said. Giving us a once-over. This is perfect. When you drive, maybe it's better if you aim for the angel.

It certainly *seemed* perfect, at that moment, and I didn't want to delve too deeply into the workings of her well-reasoned plan, so I nodded.

She opened the back door. Get out, she said to her brother. I went back and forth in my mind on whether the two of them had blood relations. He held up his bound wrists, which I hadn't seen before.

Well, untie him, she told me. And remove the gag.

I got out of the car and went over to untie him, as I was instructed. The water man looked at me through his glasses, and

I could tell he was trying to make a decision, size me up. I tried to be as inscrutable as possible, for Lydia's sake, as I loosened the handkerchief gagging him, and then the bands around his wrist. My hands sank into his wrists by just a little bit. I recoiled. The man stood up, sliding out of the car. I stepped back. Lydia's brother seemed almost to blend into the mist around us, so that he had a kind of halo. I noticed the angel then, and I relished the thought of driving into him, even though he had noticed our little congress.

Ready? she asked.

Am I? I said. That was a joke, I wanted to add. She was silent, waiting for me to begin. I wanted, I guess, a little more gratitude from her, some recognition of my sacrifice. But then I figured I was just being selfish. I was about to step back into the Hummer when I saw Lydia and the water man turn away and start walking toward the wall. And then the water man jumped on Lydia's back. It was stupid, I realized, to let his arms free. I should have known better, and felt horribly guilty. Even though Lydia gave the orders, I was to blame. I'm sure she felt utterly confident about her strength and his compliance.

But as he was trying to strangle her, I sat there beside the car in deep thought—just what was it about her that made me so attendant to her every whim? I thought about helping her right away, I really did. She was, however, handling him rather easily. She was, after all, Lydia.

When I was small and inchoate, a mere child, I wandered the annexed, grim factories of my youth, looking for work. I always kept my head down and sought out gross, thoughtless errands. Kind of like cleaning the grease trap. I worked in quite a few automobile factories, actually—delivering sandwiches and juices on catwalks twenty stories above the assembly lines for the snipers. Those grimy mercenaries joked about pushing me off—my bones being smelted into the workings of an Impala chassis—but I took their coins and continued on my way. In spite of the ruthless teasing, I didn't feel powerless.

Maybe I should have.

Then I snapped out of my state—Lydia was in trouble! Forget my lousy childhood! I stepped out of the car and pulled out my gun. Neither of them knew I had it. I'd forgotten that I had it, that I'd slipped it into my pocket as we were leaving my car. I really had forgotten. It was from my back seat, a snub-nosed pistol, but it could still kill. I didn't even give a warning. I aimed at the water man's head and fired.

The bullet passed through him and into Lydia's head.

After she slumped to the ground, I realized that my life was a rabbit hole looking for a rabbit. The man made out of water looked at Lydia's body, looked at me, and then started walking.

Hey! I called out behind him, thinking there'd be some kind of camaraderie or bonding moment between us. I had, after all, freed him, albeit at her orders. But he kept walking.

I looked at Lydia's body, then the Hummer, then the man who I swore was sweating away and diminishing in the hot twilight. I didn't want to stare at Lydia too much, just in case I accidentally uncovered her true face again. But I did see, through her soaked shirt, that her armor was mangled and shrunken. She must not have anticipated its failure. Was it the heat? Or the water? Her brother might have concocted a scheme to free himself during their entire journey. Or, who knew, maybe it was a desperate, blind chance that he took—to prove, once and for all, that he wasn't her sycophant, as I was.

He started sprinting toward the border. The angel moving toward us had drawn his gun, and the gun's wings unfurled.

I kept following the water man. Soon the mist completely enveloped us. I lost his trail, but I assumed the angel and gun following us had as well. Unable to see far, I stumbled around for quite a while, devoid of direction. I thought about Lydia's face— both of her faces actually—and wondered what I'd seen in them, what I'd hoped to accomplish by helping her out of a jam. I heard hissing gunshots here and there and I was afraid. The roar of the waterfall was deafening. I was afraid of getting caught in the waterfall, getting sucked down into whatever wet hell was below the earth's barren surface.

At some point when it was starting to get dark in earnest, I must have reached the border itself. Close enough to touch. I actually bumped into it, and quickly stepped back. I didn't die! The waterfall was cold and squishy and felt, I don't know, like I was touching an idea. I was pretty sure I was going to die there, that there was zero chance of home, or even my stupid pawn shop job.

Then I felt someone stroking my hair. No one was behind me who I could see. Then it stopped. For a second—a second—the waters parted in a sliver of a crevice. There was a humming sound. On the other side, I could see strange beings, with imprecise, blurry features, sitting on a hill, intently listening to music I could not hear on account of the humming, coming from instruments I couldn't see. The hills were shot with green so bright that my eyes were slain. But I couldn't stop looking. It was like looking into Lydia's actual face again, except it didn't bother me at all. There were tall grasses and thickets, and paradise's blackbirds soaring above them, between silver clouds—

Then the crevice closed. It was stupid not to jump through.

But, you know, I'm not sure that I didn't. I mean, I walked back to my Civic. I did. The Civic was there. The angel and gun were poring over the Hummer, but paid me no mind. I was miniscule compared to the other entities at work. The watery man was nowhere to be found. I was soaked and also scared. I drove back to my trailer and drank for a few days, thinking that would fix things.

And then, I went back to work. Although things were different. And still are different. Mostly little things. Mops don't work particularly well inside the store; they're always soaked. Mist comes into the shop at odd times, making the guns unusable. We've stopped selling them. My boss doesn't mind since business is better than ever. Tons of cars. A lot of people on horseback have shown up recently, so we have opened a livery next to the gas pumps. My boss gave me a raise, on account of my "valuable, noble service."

I moved out of the trailer on the edge of town and into an apartment complex.

I'm looking for a confidant, someone to follow, but no one has shown up at the store like that.

The angels and their guns are no longer fearsome to me. Several angels live in my apartment complex. They smoke a lot.

I often wonder about this—their dwelling amongst mere mortals—and I think I've finally figured it out. The angels are mere weapons—the sycophants, if you will—and the winged guns call the shots. The winged guns reproduce, follow or break customs of society, fall in love. They don't live in apartment complexes like the angels, but rather in burrows deep underneath the earth. The guns travel great distances through underground, pneumatic tubes. I had always thought these were gopher holes in the desert, but obviously I was wrong.

And so, everything that happened with Lydia makes perfect sense to me now. If you're not a gun, then you're an angel. This includes me. Lydia was probably a gun. It doesn't matter if you're made of water or not, or flesh and blood, or . . . well, whatever angels are made of. Angels are meant to do things—guard borders, build cars, safecrack waterfalls, operate cash registers. The guns, on the other hand, do what they love. They love the waterfall, and love to control it, to control who comes through.

Even now I'm not sure whose side I'm on. I only want to do the right thing, to live with what the world will give me. The question is, which world? Did I cross? That green hillside of music that I saw for just a few seconds—is it impossibly close or impossibly far away?

I want to know.

Dancing in a House

We want to go dancing, so we approach a nice Cape Cod. The house has indigo aluminum siding and an imitation oak door with a gargoyle knocker. The gargoyle is sticking out its tongue. It's nice. Once we're inside we see that the living room has plenty of floor space for what we are going to do. The floors are hardwood, a rich dark cherry, and the rugs are only throws, so it doesn't take any time at all to move them out of the way.

The beauty is, none of us have to ever bring our own stereo. It's a perk that comes with most houses: the voice of a house. We do however bring our own knapsack of CDs, because you can never trust peoples' tastes. The stereo is one of those upper middle class jobs—large but not ostentatious. There are a few boring family pictures on the wall, cluttering the future path of the sound, as well as a magazine rack, a coffee table—easily disposed of. After that happens, * goes to the kitchen to make sandwiches and ** warms up the stereo. I root through the backpack to begin things.

Enjoyment of music depends a lot—maybe entirely—on environmental conditions. Because this is a clean house, and because twilight creeps through the bay windows like ivy, I decide we should dance to Steely Dan. We all have our own tastes, and that's fine, but we all really like Steely Dan. The thing we like about Dan most is how the Eagles sing about him in _____. It's during the part when the Eagles are talking about steely knives being unable to kill animals. A heartbreaking moment in code, especially if you've danced to Steely Dan lots of times in houses, listening to dogs barking in the basement.

Everything is running smoothly, when just as * comes back from the kitchen with a plate full of peanut butter sandwiches, and ** has cued up _____, someone comes down the stairs. It's a girl, still pretty young. She must have been sleeping because she's rubbing her eyes. Her red hair is in a scrunchie, and she's wearing the sweatshirt of this band I'd never heard of. I reason that maybe she's woken from a nightmare, so seeing us in her house's living room might not be all that bad. Who knows, maybe it's an improvement.

The thing is, she looks exactly like my mother did at that age.

I'm about to say something to her when ***, who's been really quiet until now, just kind of skulking by the door, starts screaming at her that she's ruining everything, and why doesn't she just die. *** has always been a little bit unhinged, but I have to admit that at that moment I couldn't have agreed with him more, except maybe the dying part. I don't want anyone to die, especially when there's dancing about to start. But it's hard to tell that to *** when he gets going. It's hard to stop. Everything else more or less freezes. We're not used to interruptions once we're in a house. **'s hand hovers over the play button, and * is looking for a place to set down the sandwiches, as if the plate is hot.

The girl takes one good look at us and runs back up the stairs. I grab a sandwich and stand at the foot of those stairs, telling *** as he's running up to be cautious, that he shouldn't do anything he'd regret later. *** does a good job of ignoring me. Doors slam above us on the second floor. They open, they shut. I don't even hear ***'s heavy breathing anymore.

** starts the Steely Dan anyway, but it's not right. The power chords of _____ jangle instead of soothe, and there's no way for the music to enter me. It's never been *less* right, and I clench my head in my hands and shout to ** to turn the music off, that the moment's over, and if we're not lucky and careful we might never dance again.

I take the Polaroid of my mother out of my back pocket. I don't know who took it; I just kind of found it at the foot of my bed one day. The picture depicts my mother at a Laker Girl tryout, dancing in the empty Forum, eyes wide, doused in sweat and glitter, in yellow and purple stretch pants. It's the only picture I have of her where she's smiling. She didn't make the final cut.

* throws the platter of sandwiches to the hardwood. I put the picture away. Peanut butter splotches the floor, ruining it. I don't blame him. * couldn't have done anything else, and there isn't going to be any dancing anyway. I put my hand on his shoulder and head up the stairs. ** starts crying below me, but then his voice is very small as I notice other voices above me. Plush blue carpeting at the top of the stairs. I take off my shoes. I hear them in the bathroom, talking. But ***'s voice is much louder than hers. I want more than anything for the girl to be dancing with us, though I should have tried to ensure that when I had the chance to do something about it. Instead, I went along thinking that my silence was a lot more important than her well-being. Pain is not a form of dancing, though many confuse the two, no matter what type of thrashing occurs.

The doorknob to the bathroom is brass and shining so hard it's almost glowing. I try it. I can't bring her back, I know that. It's not her house, it's a girl's house, but that doesn't mean I feel bad at all for finding a fire extinguisher in my hands and aiming it at ***'s face. He's reaching down toward the girl's exposed shoulder, he's got her pinned to the toilet seat and her shirt almost off. It's good that he doesn't notice me before I blast his face with the cold jet, because I wouldn't want him hurting me or anything. His elbow accidentally flushes the toilet. He yells and tries to push himself backward, but he's really falling forward. As if he's really in the middle of a frenetic dance, moving to the guitar solo that closes out _____, because his eyes are closed and his mouth is open and his arms are going all over the place. So maybe other things can be like dancing after all. I keep squeezing.

Anyway, I don't know if there's much else to talk about. The girl runs out of the bathroom and while I'm hitting *** with the fire extinguisher I tell him not to ever, ever fuck with mom again. That she's a good person who doesn't deserve people who'll spend all their time figuring out what they can take from her. Then there's a hand on my arm. The girl's. She looks concerned. How can she know that all we wanted was a place to dance and forget who we are for a few minutes?

Seeing her face, the magnolia blood on her lip, reminds me when my mom took me to a basketball game. We were high up in the bleachers with the popcorn at our feet and the pigeons above us in the rafters. I heard the downpour rapping on the roof, wanting in. While the game droned on, I told my mom that I'd learned how to breakdance in a dream. I told her that it was very easy and that an angel in the dream told me that I had a natural body for it, that my spine was like a Slinky. Halftime started, and the Laker Girls started their routine. She turned away, and started crying, holding her palm to her face as if she was wearing a mask she wanted to tear off. Mom then said, and I will never forget this, that I was a good son, a beautiful son with many gifts, and no matter what happened she would love me until there was nothing left to give, or until the end of time, whichever came first.

The girl takes her hand off my shoulder and tells me that me and my friends (except ***, of course) should go, before her parents get back. Before she calls the police. I have no doubt she will. I tell her it's a nice house she has, and lots of children in faraway places would love to live in a house like this, and would give anything for this. She smiles. Something else has taken the dancing's place. A kind of emptiness, like the air's been knocked out of me.

I'm not scared, though. * and **, on the other hand, are shaking wrecks. Back downstairs, they're looking at me to lead them somewhere, to get them out of this mess and into a more manageable mess. I guess that's the definition of taking care of people. I don't know if I'm up to it. After what has happened in this house with *** and my mother, I don't know if I can dance again, or listen to Steely Dan again. But why should I tremble? As if this has never happened to anyone else in the history of the world? Like the old saying goes, you can check out any time you like, but you can't go home again.

Highly Responsive to Prayers

It's summer, but the air conditioning in the Super-Car is cold enough to kill tropical birds. I keep thinking of toucans and birds of paradise thrown into a meat locker. Not that those birds exist anymore. All the shoppers inside the SuperCar are wearing boxer briefs implanted with glowing crucifixes. They navigate between giant crankshafts. I'm wearing old-fashioned jeans and a sweater. My body's always been colder than other people's, like a reptile among mammals. I'm supposed to be meeting Fitch for lunch in the SuperCar supercafé, but he's nowhere to be found and his cell is dead. It's not necessarily a bad sign, but a *weird* one. I'm only using Fitch to get with his older sister, Abercrombie, who I've only met once. Fitch and I have been friends for about a year and I don't know him very well. But he's fine. We met at a prayer knot, both wanting some easy fundie action, not that we got any.

Abercrombie is quite simply the most beautiful girl in the entire Community. She's not at all like everyone else.

I walk past the new line of Hummer lawnmowers toward the supercafé. The lawnmowers are also designed to kill intruders. Near the entrance of the café is a banner that reads HOW WOULD JESUS FINANCE? NO INTEREST UNTIL 2029! The booths are made out of open-faced NASCAR cars, vintage nineties, and inside *those* cars, the menus are set inside these toy cars on the table. And naturally, the entire store *is* the inside of a gargantuan stock car—you enter through the headlights and the emergency exit is the exhaust. It's like a Russian doll or something. I took a year of Russian over the Internet, before the Community converted it— so to speak—to the Intranet. The old man behind the counter in the café doesn't look like he wants to be there. But maybe this is the only employment he could get. He might not even be from the Community. I order something quick because I don't want to make more eye contact with him than necessary. I also don't want to look at his sad pit crew uniform. I take my cocoabubble tea out of the café and wander a bit more.

So I walk for about fifteen minutes, watching the shoppers try to priceline a better deal for power grills and lawn phosphates, crates of frozen tamales, Persian rugs and platinum woks. Everything is big. In the back of the store is THE INTELLIGENT DESIGN CENTER, where you can order an entire house, with all the furnishings you would want (decided for you, of course). Everyone is older than me, pretty much, and wear these rings connected to their headsets with gossamer spiderwebs. They're trying *not* to look older than me. My Dad and I used to come here all the time, and he would have fit right in, before he changed.

I'm wondering whether Fitch has completely ditched me or not, when who do I see walking toward me but Abercrombie. She doesn't really belong here but I think that's why I love her. She's wearing this dress made out of an old Teflon sleeping bag, and sandals, and her eyes are as big as electrode pads. She went to real college, somewhere in the Kansan-Aleutian archipelago—not a Bible academy like I went to. She studied history, or something liberal like that. But then she had a breakdown—Fitch never told me why—and her grades tanked and she got deported back to the Community. Fitch said she was pretty crazy, but I've always wanted to help her out of her shell, if I got the chance.

Here is my chance, then.

Many shoppers stare at her, but I don't care. She's old enough, theoretically, to be my mother. Her parents had Fitch in their fifties.

When she sees me, she doesn't smile. She's been crying.

"Are you Fitch's friend Swatch?"

"Yeah. You're his sister." As if I didn't know. "Um, do you know where Fitch is?"

She grabs my elbow and she's very strong. "I have some horrible news, Swatch—it's just . . . I needed to get away from the family. I knew he was meeting you, so . . ."

"Do you want to sit down and eat?" I say.

She looks around, as if noticing for the first time that she's in a SuperCar. "You're in a SuperCar," I want to tell her while shaking her.

"Fitch is in the hospital."

"What?"

"A family ran over him. They were driving their house on the beach and they didn't see him sunbathing, and the house just pummeled him."

"Shit. Just like the Wicked Witch." How could I have said anything more asinine!

She covered her face in her hands.

"Okay," I say, taking her shoulder. It's cold. I want so much more. "So let's not eat, then?" I blurt out. Ahh!

"Where? Where could we possibly go?"

She doesn't want to be near the hospital, that much is clear. "I haven't thought that far ahead. I don't know. Someplace else in the Community, at least. Come on. Maybe we can go shooting." We move to the front door and I retrieve my gun from the coatcheck. The gun girl—she's about thirteen—looks at me kind of funny since I haven't bought anything. They always want you to buy something, as if browsing is obscene. But maybe she's just tired.

We step into the bright sunlight. To the right is the Pretzel Empire—an actual nation-state with its own post office and everything—and to the left is a mammoth, squat building, twice as large as the SuperCar, that used to be a haircare salon. But now it's empty. Above the dome it's starting to cloud up with green thunderheads.

"So . . . you sure you don't want to be with Fitch?" I say, wanting to know that we comprehend each other, that I am about to ditch him as well.

"Not right now," she says. "It seems kind of pointless, you know? He can't speak." She points to the sky, above the dome. "Look. Geese. A whole flock of them."

I see a few surveillance drones in a flock. Bird-*like*, but definitely not birds. I've never seen a goose except in pictures. But I nod anyway. I don't want to upset her. In fact, I want to kiss her extremely badly. And then I want to know how she feels.

"So where—" I begin again.

"Is that a knot?" she says, pointing to the center of the parking lot. It sure is. She starts running toward it. I had no idea she would teeter to hardcore prayer. I hear the mumbles of prayer come louder and louder as I chase her.

"Hang on . . . you don't want to—" I reach her as she reaches the edge of the knot. Maybe I'm a little embarrassed that Fitch and I used to always come to the knot to cop feels. Not that we ever got that far. The knot's guardian angel—dressed in these authentic Aramaic robes with a Tommy patch near the collar—always chased us off, thrusting his Gideon toward us, speaking in tongues. What Fitch and I did, it seems like something kids would do. It seems like a long time ago, but in some ways I still feel like a kid even though I'm fifteen.

Abercrombie edges closer to the knot and the guardian angel, who's doing his usual thing: clenching his fists, opening and closing his eyes rapidly, and looking sincere. The knot is shaped like a giant octopus, except the tentacles are just stubs. And there's a couple dozen tentacles. Anyway, you place your head into one of these stubs, and like that, you enter the Land of Light. About ten years ago, a group of churches with a big federal grant started developing these. I even remember how in grade school we had a naming contest for some of these areas in the Land of Light. All of the schools came up with suggestions, and they even made a kids show about it on PBS.

I've never done it. Like I said, it tends to mess with your mind once you're inside. They want you to accept Jesus Christ as your personal savior really, really bad and to pray all the time. And that's okay, in a way—after all, Jesus *is* my personal savior too. I'm saved, since I'm in the Community. But I guess there are different levels of being saved. And I don't want to be *too* saved, if that makes sense, like what happened with Dad.

Abercrombie starts crying again. The guardian angel gives her a bearhug. She nods as he whispers instructions into her ear, and they touch pinkies to transfer the funds. I wish it's me hugging and consoling her.

She shuffles to me. "So, Swatch . . ." She trails off.

"What the fuck are you thinking?" I ask her. I'm yelling but can't help it.

The angel hovers, steps a bit closer.

"You don't have to stay for me," she says. "Really. I mean, we don't even know each other, right?"

I'm paralyzed. She moves toward the nearest stub, slides her head inside, and with a slick pop most of her head is gone. Her body shudders and goes limp, and the guardian angel says a little prayer over her. Then he moves toward me, switching easily from pastor to bouncer mode. He's scowling. He thinks I'm a heathen. He must have good heathen radar.

"You, sinner," he barks out. "Are you ready to live before you die? To rise up after you die? Or are you going to continue your abject slide into hellfire?"

I consider holding him up, holding the entire knot hostage until Abercrombie is free, but I see the length of a pulse taser against his arm. A knife hilt is tucked into his XtremeSkechers. And those are the weapons I can *see*.

"No thanks!" I say, trying to remain calm. "I'm just going to wait over here. Until my friend's done."

"Your friend is not your friend," he says. "She's highly responsive to prayers. She—"

"Have a nice day!" I wave and walk back to the storefront. I still have a clear sightline to Abercrombie's body, which shimmers in the ozone heat. I lean against a bicycle rack. No one would ever bicycle here; it's just an antique. The SuperCar's grille gives little shade. Realistic exhaust fumes are pumped into the air around the vestibule. It helps prevent loitering, but I guess also that people have a nostalgia for carbon monoxide. I wonder what I've gotten myself into. A tiny glider swoops over the store's hood; the diamond wingtips blind me. The glider is very quiet and must be looking for intruders to the Community, those who hacked their way past the residency and credit check. Kids from Frogtown or the old bank highrises. I want to think the refugees are just like me.

Despite everything that I've been taught.

"Hey." A large hand clamps down on my shoulder. It's the old-man attendant from the supercafé. Only, instead of a pit uniform, he's wearing full riot gear. "What are you doing? Why are you loitering?" He doesn't look particularly upset at me. He's bored and has protocol to follow.

"I'm waiting for my friend." I point at the prayer knot. The guardian angel is crying, reading the prophet Amos from his Gideon. For a second I really believe he wants to help people. "Aren't you supposed to be processing vegetables or something?"

He snorts. "They have us double shifted," he says in a low voice. The low voice is smart. There are spyroaches everywhere, small as thumbs and just as dirty. "Fuckers, I don't even have a piss break except every four hours. Yuen just went up and quit and—" His back straightens. Maybe he got a call from a superior to deal with me. "Anyway, you can't stay here on the grounds."

"But my friend—"

"What your friend's doing could take a long time."

I bite my lip. "How long?"

"All night. And you don't have all night. Listen," and his voice drops again, as if down a mineshaft. "I wouldn't expect the knotters to let her up for air for a while. But look—" He points to the arched windows of the café. "It's off-peak, so you should be able to find a window table pretty easily. If you buy something, you're not doing anything illegal."

I check my gun in again—the gun girl doesn't notice me and I'm a little hurt—and seat myself near the window. The place is casual dining, everyone is too nice for words. It's a decent sightline to Abercrombie. I'm all about sightlines. The security guard/prep cook is right. Abercrombie doesn't come up for air. I spend the hours eating and drinking, whatever they have to offer—country-fried shitake, mostly. It's starting to get dark, the dome reflecting ghostly shadows onto the asphalt. The streetlamps flicker on. I wonder if Abercrombie's starting to get hungry, whether I could give her any food or drink.

I start to doze, and dream my own version of the Land of Light. Well, it's more like a half a dream, since I know I'm dreaming. Does that count? It's almost pitch black in my Land of Light, and other people run past with flashlights in their hands, laughing. I have no flashlight. There's an ocean nearby, or maybe a lake, because I hear waves and birds squawking. I hear a whispering voice next to my ear, and I wonder if it's Jesus. Then I startle awake, and I see outside that a sparkling white crusader van has pulled up next to the knot. I jump up. The dining room is full, and nearly everyone looks at me.

"Hey!" I yell. I start running toward the door. The old man looks up from the pit crew, in the middle of overturning a slab of hickory ribs. I know he's contemplating changing back into his riot gear, but then figures it's more trouble than it's worth.

Outside the door, sprinting toward the van, I see that the guardian angel moves to Abercrombie. She's still in the knot. He takes hold of her elbow. He closes his eyes and starts praying again. Then he starts up with the crying again. Crying is a lot like speaking in tongues, it seems like. People in white suits—containment suits, it seems like—move out of the van and start plucking people from the knot. They're checking some kind of meter next to each person that I hadn't noticed before. Abercrombie's meter has a gold glow. It would have been impossible to see in daytime.

Stupid stupid me. I'd heard about this happening—choosing a few who respond really well to the knot and taking them away for "further ministerial training."

Then the thought crosses my mind: maybe Abercrombie *wanted* to come to the knot in the first place. But, I don't know, felt some *obligation* to see me first and tell me about Fitch because I'm his friend.

I can't bear that thought, so I push it away.

"Leave her alone!" I shout. I'm shrill, I know this. The guardian angel smiles at me, as if to say, what do you think about this? What would you give to be me? Then he turns away and motions to a driver of one of the vans. The van pulls up.

This is illegal, right? I think. *This isn't even sanctioned by a proper church, right?*

I reach toward my gun but I don't have it; in my rush, I forgot to pick it up from coat check. My hands feel small. One or two other knotters besides Abercrombie are ferried to the van. The angel slides Abercrombie's head out of the knot. Her hair is slick from whatever is inside of there. She's gurgling. I start rushing for him then, I don't care how many weapons he has. But then I hear a "let go of her" from behind me. The old man. He *is* in riot gear. I put my hands up and turn around, but he's pointing the gun at the guardian angel, not me.

"Do you have permits?" he says.

The guardian angel laughs.

"Permits, please," the old man says, "Presbyter Knot Protocol 5. I'm also going to have to see the maintenance records of the knot *and* your vehicle."

"You have no authority," the guardian angel says.

"You're on private property, and private property is sacrosanct."

Abercrombie is looking back and forth between the two men. I try to creep forward but can't find a way to reach her .

The guardian angel looks back at the van, and then smirks, and he reaches for his taser. But the old man shoots. My bones rattle from his recoil. The angel is pushed back, body convulsing. His Aramaic Tommy robes stiffen, absorbing the bullet, and he is gathered into the arms of his deacons. He won't die; he has too much faith in himself to die. The van drives away, and Abercrombie falls toward me. I catch her. She smells like apricots and dog piss.

"Get out of here," the old man says to me, not looking at my eyes. "Just get out of here." He is pretty much in deep shit, I know that, but I don't think. I take his advice and run.

They say that in the Land of Light, you can go anywhere you want to go, and be anyone you want to be. But I know that's not true. When inside, they make you think that you want to go to the places they provide—mostly in the Holy Land. They make you think that the avatars they provide are the most amazing available. Which they are, from a purely technical standpoint.

But here's the thing, I'm not sure it's really worth it. It sounds kind of boring, except for maybe the sex. They don't *admit* this on TV, but this is what they use to lure people in. And they don't *call* it sex, of course. It's "intimacy." The relationship you have with Jesus gets kind of ... heavy, if you're a girl. And that spills over into how the girls see guys there. It's really messed up. Yeah, there *are* plenty of beautiful fundie girls there looking for guys who have accepted Christ like they have. In the Land of Light, girls are told to imagine their "future husband." To hold such an imaginary person in her heart, until he could be found in the Land of Light.

But the sense I got was that it would always be a ménage à trois, even if you get married with one of the girls, and have more kids than you could count.

After which, they figure that you'll be willing to listen to anything thrown at you. Which is maybe true, for some people.

Like my Dad, for one. I learned a lot about the Land of Light
after he kept going to the knot over and over again. He kept trying
to convince my mom and I to dive in, feel what he was feeling,
which was apparently the Holy Spirit. Then one day, he probably
decided he loved Jesus more than us and left for the Alabama Prin-
cipality. I kept going through all of his old college books after he
moved; Mom wanted to throw them away, but I hid them in the
old wine cellar. (Plenty of room there after the Community turned
dry.) I kept reading about the outside world, the way the world
used to be, trying to find Dad there. But he wasn't in those books
anymore. He was part of the Light.

I have to admit on one sick level that it's tempting. Everyone
smiling and considerate. Everyone praying, and saying how Jesus is
doing an A-OK job in their eyes. But then, the Land of Light never
leaves you. They say this is a good thing, proof of your faith. But
then you see things on the edges of sight. You're not in *control* of
what you see anymore.

And then the nasty, unending guilt comes. Which is also engi-
neered, of course.

Which the churches would tell you would be the *point.*

In that regard, I try to think of my Dad as little as possible.

Abercrombie's in the back of my Hummer5. There's an obscene
amount of room back there. I wonder if the SuperCar itself can chase
after us. She's coming to, writhing around, eyes half-closed. "Where
am I?" she mutters. It's not entirely clear she's speaking to me.

"You're in a vehicle," I say. I check out of the gates of the Shopping Center. A flock of silver drones swarms above me, then flies
to the scene of the shooting. I am harmless.

"A vehicle." She laughs. "Where are we driving to?"

"To the hospital. To see your brother."

She pauses for a long time, and for a while I think she's asleep. But then she sits up straight and says, "Jesus, is that you? Is that you driving?"

"No. It's Swatch. Your friend Swatch."

She laughs. "Stop messing with me, Jesus. Now get back here like you promised."

There is a rest stop ahead. With picnic tables and a copse of trees. The gate is closed and chained. No one uses these anymore. No one has picnics anymore. It would be easy to stop there. To rest. To get the courage to turn around and help the man who shot the angel.

"I'm your lamb, Jesus, just like you told me . . ."

My hand hovers on the turn signal, but then goes back to the wheel as we pass the rest area. I turn on the radio and try to find her a channel that will calm her down. But then I realize I'm trying to find a station to drown her out. Gospel, maybe. The blues. Something lonely. But none of the music on the radio is lonely anymore. My Dad really loved the blues before he went away.

At this point, static would do.

We pass low-lit shantytowns and trashcan fires along the river that used to be marshes, marshes that were once home to all those geese. Maybe those were the geese Abercrombie saw.

"Where are we going again?" she says.

"To the hospital. To see your brother Fitch."

"Who?"

Then she starts laughing again.

That's when I start praying. I start talking to God in a way I never have before. The words fall out of my mouth, and I don't even know what I'm saying. My head is light and I'm not even asking God for anything. Nothing at all. I'm just letting him know that I'm here, and that I have no idea who I saved, who I didn't save.

Stick Walking Fires

On All Hallows' Eve Eve, Parka sat on his motorcycle in the unending desert. The moon was a low-hanging fruit. The blue fires of Casino were off in the far distance to the north. Parka pulled an apple out of his jacket pocket, cut it in half with his claw, and offered one half to his fellow traveler Jar.

"The apple has a pleasing scent," Jar said before he ate it, crushing the apple into pulp with his mandibles.

"I would have to agree," Parka said.

"Where did you procure it?"

"In a house outside of Casino." He indicated the blazing pyramids and monoliths with his claw. "Two days ago. I forgot I had it. There it was, sitting on a kitchen table. Red and perfect." When he finished eating the apple, Parka brushed off a posse of stick insects that landed on his shoulders.

"Hey, cool, walking sticks," Jar said, brushing them off Parka's jacket.

"Is that what the locals call them? I just don't know where these bugs come from," Parka said.

"They are everywhere," Jar said, cleaning his mandibles with his fingers afterward.

Parka watched the walking sticks rattle on the hard desert ground.

"All right," Parka said, kicking his motorcycle to life. The reactors shot into clutch for a second and then hummed. Jar followed with his. "Santa Fey then?"

"They are expecting us."

Parka patted his satchel, the one containing the Amulet of Ruby Webs, which he had extracted from Casino at great cost.

"Yes they are. I do not expect traffic. Nor to encounter those we disposed of."

Parka was thinking of the Worm-Hares.

"Not under the mountains."

"Nope."

Parka leaned forward and his bike shot forward. Jar soon followed. After they broke the sound barrier, Parka put on his headphones. He liked Toby Keith.

In the great tunnel underneath the mountains, they stopped at a rest stop. They hydrated and Jar sulfurized his joints. There were a couple of other travelers at the rest stop. Others sped by on their motorcycles and flaming chariots. Every once in a while there would be a rumbling sound that would shake the wire grating of the low roof and send dust to the ground. Once there was a low growl far above, like a brane gun backfiring.

"What's that?" Jar asked once.

"Taos," Parka said, not looking up from his hammock and his well-thumbed copy of *The Toby Keith Review*.

"Ah," Jar said, going back to his sour acupuncture.

The human child who was indentured to the rest stop looked up from his abacus. He had a name tag that said SHARON. "They've been going like that for a fortnight. The Black Rooster Company is finally yielding their fortress against the Azalean Gullet."

But the two couriers ignored him. Blushing, the child went back to his figures.

"Say," Parka said, "what are you going to be for All Hallows' Eve?"

Jar pulled the needle from his spine and blew on the tip. "I was thinking Jack Nicklaus."

"Really? I love *As Good as It Gets!*"

Three of Jar's eyelids quivered, a sign of confusion and then mild amusement. "No, not the actor. The golfer."

Parka raised his eyebrows. "Really? Do you golf?"

Jar shrugged. "Who are you going to be?"

"Dwight D. Eisenhower," Parka said without any hesitation.

"Really? I love World War II!" It took Parka a few seconds to realize Jar was being a sarcastic mimic.

Parka sighed.

"But seriously," Jar said, perhaps sensing Parka's exasperation. "I would have sworn that you'd be one of the indigenous musicians." Jar pointed at the cover of *The Toby Keith Review*, in which Toby was performing in his moon-slave cage for various Being seneschals.

"I'm not quite so easily typecast, friend," Parka said. "Not quite so easily in one box or another. I have a lot of interests."

"Uh-huh," Jar said.

"Anyway," Parka said, wanting to change the subject a bit, "it won't matter if we can't make Santa Fey by tomorrow."

"Ha ha," Jar said. "Don't worry. We're in the slow season. We're deep underground. The winds of war are incapable of blowing upon our faces."

"I am not quite so sanguine," Parka said, closing his magazine and hopping off the hammock. "We should go."

"So soon?" Jar said. "I still need to sanitize my needles." He held a glinting needle out. The tip wavered.

Parka was going to say something clever and lewd but the sound of an approaching caravan drowned out any coherent thought. Three motorcycles and a black Camaro. They were slowing down and resting at the rest stop.

"Hey. Jar," Parka shouted, before the caravan stopped.

Jar looked over. It was a caravan of Casino dwellers, all Worm-Hares.

"Ugh," Parka said. "Like I said, let's go."

"Hey!" the prime Worm-Hare said, slithering out of the Camaro. It was too late. "Hey!"

"What?" Parka called out.

The other Worm-Hares had hopped off their motorcycles and were massing together. The prime pointed at the Amulet of Ruby Webs that was half-hidden in Jar's satchel. "I believe you have something of ours!" he said.

"It's not yours anymore," Jar said. "So you should have said, 'I believe you have something of yours!'"

Parka had to shake his head at this. Even in danger, he had trouble not to break out laughing. This, at least, gave them a couple of seconds while the Worm-Hares tried to parse this out.

"The Amulet of Ruby Webs is a sacred symbol for our community through many generations and systems," the prime said.

"Well, it's your fucking fault you brought it down from orbit then."

The prime paused. The other Worm-Hares were getting antsy, stroking their floppy ears with their tentacles. They likely surmised that Parka and Jar would be difficult to slay in close-quarters combat. Or perhaps they were worried about damaging the Amulet.

"How about we race for it?" the prime said brightly.

"No, you can't have a good race in the tunnel and you know that," Parka said. "Hm, I will kickbox you for it though."

All of the Worm-Hares laughed as one. "Seriously?" the prime said. "Um, okay. Sure."

"Great. If I win you'll have to leave us alone. And . . ." Parka thought about it. "Give up driving your Camaro for a year. No, wait, you'll have to give it to him." He pointed to the human child. "Aw yeah, that's right. Are you ready?"

The prime nodded and smiled, but then grew grim. "But, listen. Hey. I'm being serious here. Whatever you do, do not—*do not*—touch the red button on the center of the amulet. Okay?"

"Yeah, don't worry," Parka said dismissively. "I'm no amateurish idiot.

"Fair enough," the prime said. "I am going to enjoy kicking your ass." The residents of Casino were known for their kickboxing prowess, and the Worm-Hares learned such local arts after they followed the Beings down to the surface.

"You sure?" Jar said to Parka, putting his hand on Parka's shoulder as he was doing stretches.

"Not really," Parka said. "But, this is the only way they'll stay off our ass. So we can make it to Hallows' Eve."

Jar nodded. "Right. Hey, look at that kid's face."

Parka looked over. It was beginning to fill with walking sticks. Circling the neck, darting down the cheeks. The child was fearful, but was unable to brush the insects off, because of the chains.

"What is *with* that?" Parka said, as he stepped into the make-shift kickboxing ring, an enclosure of the Worm-Hares' motorcycles. "Seriously, do any of you know what is going on with those insects?" He pointed to the human. None of the Worm-Hares paid Parka any mind. The prime took off his leather jacket and Parka did the same. Then the Worm-Hares—and Jar too, for that matter—counted down to ten and the kickboxing match began.

Parka then entered a trance-like state, without his consent or volition. When he snapped out of it, the prime Worm-Hare was sprawled on the asphalt, his head twisted backward, tentacles twitching here and there.

"Wow," Jar said. "What happened?"

"I have no idea," Parka said. "What *did* happen?"

"He tried to kick your face, but you spun away. Then you kicked his face."

"Oh." Parka felt a few of the walking sticks scurry and drop off his shoulders, which felt sore. He didn't realize that they had landed on him. The other Worm-Hares were motionless and scared.

As Parka and Jar drove away, they noticed that the human child's body was entirely covered in the walking sticks. Parka tried to make eye contact, as a way of saying, Hey, the Camaro's yours, I hope you get to drive it someday, but there were no eyes visible to connect with.

A few hours later in the tunnel, they had to stop again. Flashing lights and a tall human woman wearing a sandwich board.

"Bypass," the woman said.

"Oh, fuck me," Parka said.

"Cave-in," the woman elaborated. She also had a name tag that said SHARON. "You'll have to go to the surface."

"You think?" Parka said.

"Hey, she's just doing her job," Jar said.

"I know that, Jar," Parka said. "And don't lecture me, like I'm some kind of phobe. I mean, I'm the one who gave a Camaro to a human child. I'm a friend of these people, believe me."

"Whatever you say," Jar muttered.

"Fuck," Parka said, trying to focus. "Let's see, we're about three hours away from Santa Fey by the tunnel. But who knows now. Is it hot up on the surface?"

The woman was about to say something, but she was drowned out by a quaking roar from above, and then a series of blossoming explosions.

"Well, I guess that answers your question," Jar said.

"Okay," Parka said. "I hate this. We're going to miss Hallows' Eve."

"Stop whining," Jar said. "The Amulet is the important thing, remember? Priorities?"

"I wish I had more apples," Parka muttered, revving his motorcycle and easing into the detour that the woman directed them to. He meant to ask her about the walking sticks.

Parka's and Jar's motorcycles climbed to the surface. The surface was full of bright light, and wispy ash was in the air. The couriers were in the desert foothills. An Old Being was hunkered down, sprawling in the desert. Eagle-falcon drones—it was hard to tell what mercenary company they were attached to—swooped toward, bombed, and soared away from the Being. Parka and Jar stopped and assayed the narrow road ahead, and where the road stopped.

"Ugh," Parka said. "The Being's in the way."

"Yeah."

The Being ate mountains. Finishing those, the Being would move to the badlands and mesas. Sparks shot off its slimy, translucent fur as it swept its mammoth pseudopods across sheep farms and little casinos. There were kites on stiff strings protruding from its upper reaches. When the Beings landed on a planet and sucked out the nitrogen, galactic civilizations would follow. After a few years, the Beings would be full, and then calcify, leaving several seedling Beings in its wake, who would then transport themselves to new systems. And *then* the residue of the Being's wake could be properly and safely mined. This residue powered the vast interstellar transmutation ships. Until that time, there would be war around the perimeters of the Beings, dozens of mercenary guilds and free companies jostling for position.

"There's no way we can drive around it?" Jar asked.

"Too many gullies." Parka put on his telescopic sunglasses and squinted at the Being. "Well, it's possible to . . . no."

"What?" Jar said. "Tell me."

More ships screamed above them, fast-eagle merlins that carpetbombed a trench right in front of the Being. Prisms trailed in the bombs' wake. Counterfire from the trench screamed upward.

"We'll jump *over* said Being," Parka said.

Jar started laughing so much that sulfur tears started streaming out of his ducts, splashing upon his upholstery. "Whither the ramp, friend, whither the ramp?"

"What, you can't do a wheelie?"

"No . . . I've—I've never tried."

"And where did you learn to ride again?"

Jar paused. "On the ship."

"Fuck, no wonder. You have to learn on the surface. I learned in Tennessee, before its flattening. Everyone wheelied. Well, anyway, it's easy. You just have to utilize the booster with the correct timing. You want to practice?"

"No, I'll watch you first."

"Are you scared?"

"Yeah."

Parka leaned forward and put a claw on Jar's carapace. "Well, don't be. OK, let me make my approach."

Parka put his motorcycle in reverse about a half a kilometer and considered his approach, licking his lips. Jar crossed his arms and looked back and forth from the Being to Parka. The Being began humming, with resonances of local accordion noises. Parka leaned forward, kicked his motorcycle on, and then roared forward, shooting past Jar in an instant. Then Jar turned on his motorcycle as well, and revved, and soon enough was a few lengths behind Parka.

"No, Jar!" Parka shouted, looking behind him. But there was no way for Jar to hear him, both traveling at the speed of sound. The Being was before him. Through its diaphanous surface, Parka could see about a thousand humans, and also four hundred birds of various types, five herds of cattle, a parking lot of used cars, several giant tractors, many boulders/reprocessed mountains, broken casinos and a few off-worlders who were too stupid to get out of the way.

Parka hunkered down and wheelied and hit the booster. He soared, gaining clearance by a few meters over the Being. There were white kites protruding from the gelatanious skin of the Being, the kites' strings puncturing the surface and spooled far below. The eagle-falcons' bombs had accidentally scarred the Being in many places, but they weren't able to break through the surface.

When the booster gave out, Parka held out his arms and leaned forward, just clearing the Being. He skidded to a halt and spun the motorcycle around, watching Jar.

Jar had accelerated too late, and he seemed to hang over the Being, suspended like one of the eagle-falcons.

Jar gave a thumbs up sign.

Then one of the kites snapped to life and whipped at one of his legs, and the thread tangled around the limb. Jar careened forward and separated from his cycle, which slammed against the surface of the Being's skin—the booster still on—and ricocheted upward. With the booster still going at full capacity, the motorcycle slammed into the wings of one of the low-flying fast-eagle merlins that was overhead. The eagle-merlin spiralled out of control and careened into the side of a mesa about ten kilometers away. Parka felt the back blast as he watched Jar try to pull at the kite string, tearing at the ashy paper. But the thread held. He landed, almost gently, on top of the Being. He tried to stand up, but in a few seconds he was beginning to sink into the Being.

"Jar!" Parka shouted. "Hang on!"

"Sorry," Jar shouted back, his legs already consumed. He looked down. "There's some serious alternate reality shit going on in there," he said.

"Keep fighting!" Parka said, but he knew it was hopeless.

Jar held up all of his arms and slid into the Being.

Parka hunched over his motorcycle, his head sinking between the handlebars. About a dozen walking sticks landed in his fur. He ran his claw over the hair, scooping them up and eating them. They tasted like Fritos.

"Nasty," he said, spitting them out.

He started riding again to Santa Fey in silence, with the shriek of the pre-mining operational maneuvers above him and to all sides. He put on his Toby Keith but even this wouldn't soothe his guilt.

When he saw Santa Fey on the horizon, and the glow of the madrigal lights along the city walls, and the faint thrum of fiddles and cymbals and electric guitars, he became light-headed and also ridden with shame, which was far worse than guilt. He stopped his motorcyle and revved it, his gills fluttering.

At last he thought of Jar and also tried to consider what his life meant, in the end.

"Fuck it," he said, and he turned around, back toward the Being.

About a kilometer away, Parka stopped and took the Amulet out of the pouch. He knew, whatever happened, that his diplomatic career would be over. He would never be able to set foot in Santa Fey again, and they would in all likelihood hunt him down, if he lived. He would likely have to leave the planet he had grown fond of. Slowly, he slid the Amulet around his neck. The walking sticks rose to the occasion, then. Soon there were thousands congregating around him, wedged in his joints and lining his shell. They felt warm and they tickled. The Being gurgled in the distance.

He remembered, with a sudden pang, what he had forgotten at the time—that the walking sticks were in his joints in much the same way during the kickboxing match.

A Camaro pulled up beside him, revving its engine. The boy, Sharon, was driving it; he was still covered in insects. Actually, Parka couldn't tell whether there was a boy there at all. Parka's own insects dropped off him and scurried up the car and through the open window to be with Sharon.

"Get in," insect boy said. His voice was deep and unwavering.

Parka turned off his motorcycle and parked it, and then got in the Camaro. He was nearly too tall for it, but he bent his head forward. He saw that the sandwich board was in the back seat.

"How did you get free of your post?" Parka said.

"Liberation takes many guises," Sharon said, revving the engine. "Enslavement is the pure heart of industry."

"Alrightey," Parka said.

Sharon turned toward him. "Therefore you shall be the Dwight D. Eisenhower of enlightenment and camaraderie."

The Camaro shot forward, and Parka fumbled for a seat belt. But there was none. They were driving right toward the Being. Parka was beginning to think this was a bad idea.

"I have an idea," Parka said. "How about we kickbox? If I win, you have to stop the car."

But the boy ignored him, and continued to accelerate. A few of the walking sticks from the boy scurried onto Parka's arm. He was too afraid to swat them away.

"Seriously," he said as much to himself as Sharon, "there has to be some underlying plan to this endeavor."

Sharon didn't turn as he said, "Not really. No."

They shot toward the Being, which soon was their entire horizon. The walking sticks were rattling with the velocity. The Amulet was hot against his carapace. Parka closed his eyes.

In a blink of his outer eyelid, he expected one of three conclusions to his current predicament.

The first involved a high-impact collision against the outer husk of the Being, flattening him and the beautiful Camaro.

In the second, the Camaro would puncture the Being's skin and come to some kind of high-impact collision *inside* the Being, with any number of the farm animals, people, and other physical remnants of the aboriginal civilization surrounding him and either flaying him or welcoming him into a pathetic intra-Being community.

In the third, Sharon would halt at the last second, or dodge the Being somehow, because he was really trying to fuck with Parka's head, which he was doing a spectacular job with already.

He missed home all of the sudden, the home he had tried so hard to forget, his twenty parents who all had contradictory advice for his well-being, and who hated interstellar travel—

"It won't be long," Sharon muttered, and then the Being was upon them, and they were upon the Being, and the Camaro screamed. It really screamed as it blew through the outer shell of

the Being, causing an explosion in its wake and argent and vermillion sprays all around the car, and strands of Being fur flying.
The front windshield shattered and the pieces blew away like tiny
feathers. Then the top of the car ripped off.

They were inside the Being. But the Camaro didn't stop. In
fact it seemed to gain an extra level of speed once it was inside
the Being. The walking sticks glowed like solar flares or brane-
gun bullets from a galactic transmutator. Past the blue and green
haze, Parka couldn't see much—shapes moving around that were
vaguely aboriginal in form. The only thing he could see clearly
were the local sorcery-powered vehicles that were known as "monster trucks." They raced toward the Camaro, dozens of free-float-
ing kites strung to their menacing hulls, but they were far too slow
to reach the rocketing, black Chevrolet stock car. The inside of the
Being smelled like ferrous oxide, phlegm, sinew, and transdimen-
sional energy. Before he was able to formulate the thought to look
for Jar at all, the Camaro had burst through the other side of the
Being with a roar. More fine, plush incandescent Being fur surrounded them. Then the light grew sharp and bright, and Parka
shielded his eyes.

When he moved his pincer away from his face, he saw that
the Camaro was sailing in the air above a deep canyon, which the
Being was on the edge of.

"I want to warn you," Sharon said, "that you might want to
brace yourself."

The Camaro seemed to be suspended above the dry riverbed
far below for a few seconds, and slowly began to arc down. The
other side of the gully seemed impossibly far away. The walking
sticks, still glowing, began to thrum.

And then Parka touched the button on the center of the Amulet,
the one forbidden thing. The red rays embedded in the metal burst
out, and solidified into strands many meters long, following the
contours of his arms. Then they ballooned out like wings.

They *were* wings.

Without really thinking—and it might have been the Amulet thinking for him—he stood up and stretched his arms out. The wings were massive, and the Camaro wobbled but righted itself. As it fell, Parka could hear the Being on the other side of the canyon shrieking, and feel its reverberations around his neck.

Parka leaned forward and the Camaro landed right on the edge of the canyon with a thud. Sharon hit the brakes and the Camaro spun around. The Being was, in fact, in the throes of dying. Eagle-merlins from above were trying to maneuver out of the way, but aquamarine slime burst out of the Being like sulfuric geysers and coated the carpetbombers, which spun around and veered wildly. Parka could hear a high, sonorous call from many miles away—the continental emergency siren from Santa Fey.

Sharon was still. But then he pointed forward.

The Worm-Hare posse was there, gathered around a minivan, each with a brane gun strapped to its arm.

"You've *got* to be kidding," Parka said. He tried to get out of the car, but it was difficult because of his nascent wings. He ended up crawling forward through the glassless windshield and onto the hood. The wings settled around him like a reptilian cape.

"We want our car back," the prime Worm-Hare said. It was a different prime from the one Parka had defeated in kickboxing. The sliding door of the minivan was open, and Parka could see the original prime in the back of the minivan in a shimmering heal-sac. "To say nothing about the Amulet, one of the key symbols of our people, which you've gone on and fucked up as well. You know that your corporation is going to hunt you down for triggering 'dragon mode,' right?"

Parka laughed. *Dragon mode.* "That's great. Anyway, you seem to forget that I won the car fair and square. I don't know why you're so upset about that, considering your current sweet ride."

"We don't care," the prime said, hoisting his gun at Parka, ignoring the jab about the Honda Odyssey. "We just want a souvenir to take back with us off-world." He indicated the dying Being in the distance. "This planet is a cursed cesspool. There's nothing here anymore. But nothing would make us happier than to disintigrate your sorry carapace and take this car into orbit with us."

Parka spread his wide wings—which didn't hurt at all—because he thought it would scare them. But it didn't, at all. He sighed. He realized that sometimes the smallest moments could change a creature's life. He had given the Camaro to a human as a prize, and had thought nothing of it. But here he was, about to die from the Worm-Hares after all, and with weird wings. But all the same, he felt good about his generosity, even if Jar wasn't there to share it with him.

With that in mind, he wasn't going to back down.

Sharon was motionless, but then he looked in the backseat and started laughing. It was such a quiet, tinny laugh that it shocked everyone into stillness.

"What?" the prime Worm-Hare said, exasperated. Then there was a red dot on his spiny forehead. Parka stared at it.

"Will someone *please* tell me what's going on?" the Worm-Hare said.

Then there was a whooshing sound, and a crossbow bolt hit the Worm-Hare's forehead where the red dot was. The bolt went through his head, blasting into the front windshield of the minivan. The prime slumped over.

Parka turned around. There was someone in the back seat.

"Hey," Jar said, sitting up, slinging a laser crossbow over his shoulder and looking groggy.

"Christ on a—" Parka said, but he stopped, because he didn't know what to say. Instead, he ran to Jar and wrapped his leathery, demonic wings around his friend in a familial embrace.

"Look at you," Jar said, still sleepily. "With wings and shit."

"It's the Amulet," Parka said. The remaining Worm-Hares were forgotten, but they had made their pathetic escape in the minivan. "But, anyway, priorities. How the hell did you get there? You weren't there all along, were you?"

Jar shrugged. "No, not really. I was in the Being and then . . . um, I don't remember much about that, but I saw this sweet Camaro cruising through, and then stop in front of me, and I said to myself, hey, maybe I should hop on board, so I did. And I must have picked up this crossbow. I guess I was on a shooting range for a while or something?"

Parka had no recollection of the Camaro slowing down enough for anyone to jump aboard.

He disengaged from Jar. "I'm just glad you're safe."

"Well, you came back, friend. That's the important thing. I'd still be in there without you."

"The Tree requests your presences," Sharon said.

"What?" Jar said.

"Ah, the kid, he's like that," Parka said. He waved toward Sharon. "Okay, okay, the Tree. But first, we need to get a beer."

Later that day Jack Nicklaus and Dwight D. Eisenhower and Sharon met for a summit over a few of the local beers.

"How's things?" Jack said.

"Super," Dwight said.

"Awesome," Jack said.

Sharon was silent. They were in a basement tavern some-where north of Albuquerque, at a circular table. It was the off-season, and likely everyone in a 500 kilometer radius was trying to flee the potential blast zone of the Being, so they had the place to themselves. The beer was warm but the off-worlders didn't care. Sharon didn't order anything so Parka had the bartender make him an Arnold Palmer. Toby Keith was playing on the speakers and everything was all right with the universe, at least for a few minutes.

"I'm going to miss Hallows' Eve with the gang," Jar said. "But it's a small price to pay."

"Yeah, it would have been fun. I'm glad we dressed up anyway."

"You know, I wonder if Eisenhower would have won the war faster if he had wings like yours."

"It's very possible," Parka said. The Amulet against his chest pulsed like a second heart. The walking sticks swirling around Sharon clicked and skittered.

"What do you want to do after we, er, look at some tree that might very well be imaginary?" Parka said.

"I don't know," Jar said, taking a sip of his Budweiser Light. "It's hard to say. Go back home, maybe. Start over with a new corporation. How about you?"

"Well, maybe I'll stay here," Parka said. "I haven't decided. But I like it here. I still have no idea what the fuck happened."

"With the Amulet?"

"A little. But mostly with the Camaro. And the Being."

"Ah, that's understandable," Jar said.

Parka leaned forward, which was awkward because of his wing span. "What I want to know is . . . I might not never understand, ever, what's going on with these walking sticks. But they're trying to say something, trying to do something. They're trying to survive on this godforsaken planet we—I mean, not us personally, I mean the mining ventures—fucked up for resource management. And for what? So we can get more fuel for our transmutators to find more planets to fuck over and destroy?"

Parka was melancholic, but not just for geopolitical reasons. He realized that this might be one of the last times of relative normalcy with his good friend.

"Yeah," Jar said. "You make a good point. Maybe I'll stay too. And learn how to properly ride a motorcycle and do a wheelie." He laughed and then downed his beer. "Come on, Sharon," he said. "Finish your drink."

They rode for an hour in silence through the empty desert, and could see the Tree from many kilometers away. A towering, shadowy shape. Sooner rather than later—Sharon wasn't exactly following a speed limit—they could see the enormity of the living structure. Parka stood up in the car, letting his body poke out of the shorn top, letting his wings free.

"Holy shit," Jar said.

The Tree was as tall as the highest peaks that the Being had dessicated, many kilometers high. And the Tree was on fire. Smokeless fire. The tree pulsated with orange light. The branches were leafless, but they spiraled in gargantuan yet intricate patterns.

About a thousand meters away, Sharon stopped the car. Everyone got out. The walking sticks encompassing Sharon, or perhaps embodying him, were glowing in syncopation with the Tree. Then it became clear that the Tree was made up of billions of the walking sticks.

There were many other abandoned vehicles all around the Tree in a ring.

"Why are the walking sticks doing this?" Jar whispered.

Parka shook his head but didn't say anything. He had no idea.

Sharon turned to the two of them and said, "We need you two, the Dwight D. Eisenhower and Jack Nicklaus of interpersonal diplomacy, to carry a message back to your people. You will relay terms for peace." Sharon began walking toward the Tree.

"Wait, Sharon," Parka said. "What will happen if we do?"

"What will happen if we don't?" Jar said.

Sharon paused for a second and said, "My name's not Sharon." Then he began walking toward the Tree again.

Parka watched him for a little while, and looked at Jar, who shrugged.

"Who the hell knows," Jar said.

As the general and the golfer followed Sharon to the base of the Tree, Parka swore he heard Sharon, who wasn't in fact Sharon, humming a tune, one of Toby Keith's more recent songs about exile on the moon and earthly liberation. Or maybe it was only the sound of the walking sticks and the desolate wind making music together, which wasn't meant for a stranger like him, wasn't for him to understand.

ing The Flower-Ape

I sprinted through the translucent tube with the curfew avatar slithering behind me. I had a date that night with Kathy at the Flowering Ape, and I wasn't going to be late for him. Even if kissing him never materialized.

I could hear the avatar hiss. The foot traffic was light in the tube, just a few drunken lovers laughing at the mega-cobra as it tried to catch up to me. The previous year, in an effort to curb truancy from the Chartering School for Young Telepaths, they'd switched from a lumbering golem-type creature to a giant cobra for patrolling the tubes between the space stations. They thought it would be "scarier," instilling fear in our young hearts. Whatever. The avatar was pokey, which was all that mattered to me.

Just as I was losing my breath, I finally saw the friendly confines of the Flowering Ape. I smelled it too. Hot taffy. Surface-distilled vodka. A perfume called Crushed Dreams. My monthly pass grafted to my pinky, I extended it and jumped inside the barrier, the door whisking me through. The cobra reached the door a couple of seconds later. Knowing it would be repulsed, it growled (a flaw in the gene design, I guess) and turned away.

I sighed, looking for Kathy, kind of glad to be there but also a little desultory. Despite its alleged function as an amusement park and semi-illicit hangout, the Flowering Ape wasn't very amusing. Its glass slides and rafters, curved with transparent spacescapes, were full of centenarians floating to the observation decks, dictating now-memoirs to their off-world agents. A lot of them were alums of the Chartering, where I was learning how to meld with the shepherds. I hadn't had the privilege of that experience yet. Sometimes it took time, my teachers always told me.

So instead of thinking on all that was troublesome, I instead found an empty pod for two and waited for my lover, Kathy. Or rather, my "lover," Kathy.

Kathy was late. He was either late or he never arrived at all— and yet which do you think I would rather have had? Waiting, I daydreamed about Kathy kissing my neck in a corner of the Ape. Maybe I'd kiss his neck too, and touch that sensitive spot on his left knee that he was always talking about. Maybe we wouldn't have gone any further—we weren't technically a couple after all—but it would have made me happy for a time, being close to someone, especially someone who seemed to like me. Maybe we'd have a drink together if we weren't too tired afterward, and talk about what telepathy all meant, and what the shepherds meant to him, to me.

Bored, I slid my pod upward, with little poofs of the anti-gravity jets, while the alums jostled their pods, racing them vertically. Shepherds swam in the vacuum above me. I saw their diaphanous edges shift around. The aliens—the reason I was in school in the first place—were powerful hypnotists, even though they really didn't mean to hypnotize. They (and we, the telepaths) made interstellar travel happen. A shepherd, with a telepath's guidance, enveloped a spaceship and sent it on its merry way across wherespace to the other planets of the Parameter.

It was a very convenient form of space travel.

I hadn't been chosen by a shepherd yet, and seventeen years old was kind of late for that kind of choicelessness, but I couldn't do anything about it happening until it *happened*. Kathy liked to talk about his shepherd Bazzarella all the time. He treated shepherds like horses, and made up names for them, and called them "boys" and "girls," though shepherds didn't have any boy or girl parts.

"Well, they reproduce, don't they?" I could hear his voice in my head, but it wasn't really him (the telepathy's only with shepherds, not with people, after all), but rather a kind of mental image I kept of him. I wasn't sure if keeping that image in my thoughts made me creepy. I wanted to argue with this Kathy-thought-projection that the shepherds weren't either boys or girls. How could they be? But then, speak of a devil, Kathy was actually at the base of the windtunnel entrance (he was a senior, and had no curfew. He might have petted the cobra on his way to the Ape). It was really him, pointing up at me, and I really didn't feel like arguing with my own thoughts anymore.

Kathy was in a black/silver dress and his beard had tons of prismed jewels embedded in the wiry hairs. The dress was slinky, I guess, but not fitting him particularly well. He waved. It was possible he was looking up my own slinky dress through the translucent pod bottom.

He waved again. I opened my mouth to shout something out at him (why did I suddenly want him, the stooge? Was it his beard and blackened dress?). But he turned around and four other students from the Chartering milled around him at the pit of the vertical tunnel, already listless. I felt like the child keeping up with the larger kids, already I felt this. At the same time, a doddering alum—easily a century and a half old—must have lost motor control, because her pod started skidding down the transparent wall-face. Outside, a shepherd came near the window but darted away again, leaving a vermillion trail. A soothing emergency light bathed everyone's face in red. Kathy's friends started laughing at the alum's loss of control.

A little cruel, a little cruel.

As the emergency crews rushed in and started resuscitating the apparently dead woman, I set the pod down and stepped out into the group—the pack?—of my fellow students that Kathy had brought along. I was disappointed in him; we talked about making out, how that could have been an important portal into a deeper type of friendship. And I wanted some privacy/solace with him, if he had any to provide. Apparently he didn't, because he'd brought along those fellows.

They didn't seem like fellows. Their gazes treated me askance, if they treated me with looks at all. I recognized them, of course, the school wasn't that big, but at the same time those people seemed to me to be as weird as shepherds, maybe moreso.

Yet they waited for me. I couldn't tell them apart, at first.

Kathy took the crook of my arm.

What made me stick around, what made me not blurt out a stupid excuse and slip away, was that Kathy sometimes said truly profound things, and I would realize weeks later that he was actually trying to be tender to me, profundity only being an afterthought. "Your hair is like a cauldron wrought from air," he said once, touching my red ends. I was waiting for a moment like that from him at that moment, but it was pretty clear he didn't want to go any further; at least, not with me. It was pretty unclear whether he ran into this pack in transit or whether this was the plan all along.

"We're going," Kathy said, more like announced, "to ride one of the shepherd ships. I thought you'd be game." I decided that it would be a good thing to nod, so I nodded. Default smirks arrived on the faces of the others.

I realized that part of that glaze on their faces was a shepherd-gaze, that each was paired with their own shepherd. I was the odd-fellow out.

"Let's go," Drexley said, hugging his fish-scaled arms. "It's cold in here. And boring." I knew his name was Drexley because his name tag said so. Below his name was a disclaimer that only FRIENDS could use his nickname "Drex." Below that was a ledger showing his exact net worth at that moment. It was lots of boon. Drexley started laughing. His voice pierced. Other names were given to me in hasty introductions: Lund, Zenith Marie, America.

This group that Kathy brought to me, then, had punctured through the barrier of telepathy and were tied to shepherds. I hadn't. How could I have said no?

I didn't want to say no.

Drexley called his shepherd Thousandhorse. Lund called his shepherd Anatolia-Blossom. Zenith Marie called her shepherd the Boxer. America called her shepherd Jackie. Boy, girl, boy, girl.

These weren't the names the shepherds gave to themselves. The gang wouldn't reveal those names to a semi-interloper like me.

We walked in a cluster, a closed fist of bodies out of the Flowering Ape. I tried to mimic their easy gait, and in the corridor, I noticed the wide eyes of the old alums, gripping drink bulbs and probably wondering, who are these people, who breathe the same air as me, so young, so very young?

And that, I had to admit, made my toes warm.

We walked to the docking bay, opposite the school. There were no cobras waiting to pounce on me there.

Along with his fishscale arms, Drexley had a fake lazy eye. Lund's teeth were coated with a substance that made them shimmer like shepherds. Zenith Marie wore a heavy belt around her thin hips (which held up pants that were like custom-made battle armor) that attached to a knot in her long coarse hair, ensuring proper balance. America had infrared sensors on the tips of her fingers. These were cultivated nuances. I guess mine was that I had no apparent quirks, no set-design to call my own.

Yet it was still hard, despite how strange they were to me, to tell the four of them apart. It was easy to notice that Kathy craved the pack. He wasn't quite a full member; apparently, he would have to ignore me a lot more to get there. They were assessing him, and so he acted louder, laughed at mild jokes a half-second too quickly and a half-second too long. But in some secret self-part that he won't let anyone see, he was shriveling, a wilting boy in a beautiful dress.

That probably made me a . . . sidekick, then. A familiar. A creature not-yet-with-shepherd summoned.

It wasn't until I was actually on one of the docked rockets that I realized they were—I mean, we were—not supposed to be there. We were trespassing and what kind of shit was Kathy getting me into?

It was a small ship, shaped like a dart, coated in mock-quicksilver. The smallest class of rockets. Outside the bridge, a couple of shepherds loomed, swirling around the ship, called the *Gray Freighter*, now that was a good sign, in slow motions. The shepherds' colors were vivid and all over the place. Then a third shepherd shot forward. Kathy's face got all scrunched, like he was concentrating on something inside of himself but also at a point, say, between his big toe and middle toe. Like there was a coin or a little toy there.

Then I realized he was talking to his shepherd, the one who had just come, Bazzarella. Soon there were five shepherds swirling around the docked ship. They were all assembled like the humans were: Thousandhorse, and Anatolia-Blossom, and yes, the Boxer, and you too, Jackie, shepherd of America. What was going to happen next? The air on the bridge smelled like ozone, as each made connections with their shepherds. I kind of felt sad for the shepherds and I shuffled my feet. If shepherds had emotions (hypothetically) I was sure they wouldn't have appreciated telepaths ascribing false identities to them, including the whole boy-girl divide.

It *was* a divide, wasn't it? I didn't know where I stood on that divide. Or maybe I was in the middle, falling into the chasm.

I wanted to know the shepherds' secret names. I didn't ask, though, and no one noticed my shuffling and moping. After about three minutes of this concentration, America whispered, grunted really: "Which of you will bait-take?"

Kathy started cackling. He spun around and around, and the others didn't seem to mind. They let that display of emotion by the neophyte pass. "Bazzarella will hitch with us."

"That's fantastic," Drexley said, unenthusiastic. Kathy touched my shoulder; a familiar but at that point vague gesture. He craned his head up and said—maybe to the vacuum, or the Parameter itself, certainly not to any of us—"What do you think my girl wants?" Girl being his shepherd. I stifled saying something to Kathy and instead gazed at all those assembled, and looked in each telepathy-occupied eye, and asked out loud what the hell was going to happen next.

They noticed me for the first time, really noticed me. Fine. That shouldn't have been that surprising. They really didn't make formal introductions in the first place. But the fact that their faces were exactly the same as before was a little disheartening. They wanted me to believe shepherds overwhelmed normal discourse for them, which was bullshit. My professors conversed with shepherds during class while chiding us to pay more attention—did we realize how important we were for the well-being of the Parameter?—and they didn't bat an eye.

America's eyes twinkled. "It's spontaneous. Everything needs to be spontaneous. We can't predict what will happen next."

"What?" I said. I looked around the bridge of the *Gray Freighter.* Kathy was shuffling toward the control crux. His shepherd was blotting out the light of the others.

"Someone's . . . one of us has stolen a series of passcodes," Zenith Marie said. "I'm not telling you which of us, because that would get any one of us into trouble. Not the least of which you." She bent her arms back and Drexley put his arm on her shoulder. He was the only one truly serious for a few seconds, and that too passed. "So we're . . . what's the word?" Maybe Zenith Marie had a dictionary implant. She tussled her blond hair and said, "Joyriding."

"I don't know," I blurted out when the cordon around me faded. They started wandering around, like blissful zombies. Lights and spherical grids engaged and started humming. Spaceship-type things started happening. I didn't move. I supposed that running away and alerting authorities would have been a strong, morally upright choice. My parents, any one of them, would have been proud of such a choice. A virtuous nectar would form on the tip of my tongue.

However, nothing of the sort happened. I downcast my eyes and gave a smirk, but stayed inside the confines of the bridge.

After we launched (my sixty-third time. I kept track of such things), Lund, up to that point silent, leaned over the makeshift couch toward me and said, "What were you smirking about before? Right before we left."

His eyes were blue. He was cute and I hated, at first, thinking that.

I said: "Because we're going to be in so much trouble that it's not worth worrying about," and that, at least, was not bluster.

We accelerated to ten percent the speed of light, the shepherd around the ship started getting brighter, and we were in wherespace, which no one could ever really see that well, because the shepherd always kind of blocked the view.

Then it dawned on me: wherespace was pretty boring. Unless you were the telepath whose shepherd surrounded the rocket, of course. Then it was all colored waterfalls of the mind and tangled nuances of shepherd-speak—not that I would have known. But for passengers without any particular place to go, well, it was like riding a planetary elevator ferry just for the sake of the ride.

Moreover, the *Gray Freighter* was pretty crummy to begin with. The walls were molded with scoured antimon residue, and the air felt full of atrophy. Or at least bacteria. The square windows were tiny, barely wide enough for me to view the shepherd aura protecting and transporting the ship through wherespace. The colors were pretty pretty, scampering yellows and mauves, but it was like being locked in a hostel with the Wang Wei Falls outside the window, with five kilometers of falling, graceful water just out of reach.

Drexley told us that it would take about three days, through some astrolabe sixth sense of his, I didn't know, to reach the Blake system.

Five hundred light years away. Whatever. More important, the gang forgot to pack much food. Now that was bright. Some crackers, some ten-year-old dehydrated gelato in the crawlspace that functioned as the "pantry."

The group of us sprawled on the curved couches on the edges of the bridge. I settled down slowly on my own couch, crossing my legs and straightening out my dress. Kathy was the only black sheep, because he had to be, in order to pilot us. This was his hour of no small glory. The shepherd-link shone in his face. The jewels coating his hair fractured and resonated, no doubt triggered by the contact by the shepherd pricking his mind, and the mind was attached to the skin and therefore his hair, wasn't it? It was all connected.

"Good girl," he kept muttering, annoyingly.

In this environment, the pack of people let some measure of their guard down. The angles of their sprawling were still artful, don't get me wrong, they were always artful. But a layer of varnish peeled off. I was always observant about other people's varnish.

America yawned and put her infrared sensor hands under the couch, as if there was a laser missile under there. Her hands, which once seemed breathtaking, now seemed vaguely stupid. But I didn't blame her much for her hands; maybe her parents insisted on them. Parents were always insisting on accessories. Zenith Marie played with the belt attached to her hair. "This is so fucking boring. Lund, tell me why we did this again?"

"We thought it would be violatory." Smart boy, he had brought a megazine to read and watch, a Persian woman reading infernok-rusher poetry.

"Violation of what? Drex? Any answers?" Zenith said, crossing her arms.

Drexley stared off into the bridge crux. "What?" he said. "Yes, exactly as you said." Drex started staring at Kathy in this really unreasonable way. Kathy was off in his own world of course. As if Drex was sizing up whatever Kathy had to give him. And it scared me to think of what Drexley might have needed.

America bit her lip and leaned her head back.

It was a maelstrom of nothing.

What did I expect—running around the halls and tagging the walls with expletives and feedback alphabets? I wasn't twelve, I was seventeen.

"Well, the least someone could have done was to bring some drugs." The voice was mine, but it didn't feel like my mind constructing these things to say, and then ordering my jaw to say them. Not at first.

"If there's no drugs, you know," my voice continued to say, "to help with staring at the shepherd, kind of like lava flows, then what's the point? Why am I here?"

And I didn't even *do* drugs or secrete them.

They all stared at me. Kathy giggled from the bow, but not at me. America started smiling, not toward Kathy but at me, and I knew I had moved myself from the void to some place not quite a void in some of their eyes.

"I'm going to take a walk to the engine room," I said. "And then find the standard-issue gelato, and try to cook something." My hands were on my hips and they were looking at me with some inner awareness of their own condition. I was like a lens. Anyone had the potential to have that effect on anyone else; all it took was a bit of practice in front of a mirror.

"Things get weird near the engine room," Drexley said, still staring at Kathy, who wasn't paying attention to any of the subtle shifts in autochthonous power structures going on, the bastard. I wanted him to be proud of me. I still didn't quite feel comfortable enough to nick Drexley's name to "Drex." "The walls are thinner there. Wherespace pours in there."

America stood next to me, stretching her arms and clapping once. "But that might be *interesting*. Come on, Drex." She was speaking to Drex but put a hand on my shoulder. It was cool, almost cold. Drexley, instead of consenting with our constitutional, remained still. But that was fine, the way a thin bandage was fine. Lund and Zenith Marie arose too. There was a mission, however simple, and I led them into the heart of the mission, however childish to Drexley's eyes.

Crawlspaces. Humming walls, shit-brown supply boxes. Motivational etchings. Very erratic gravity in places. Zenith Marie bit her lip.

What was left to discover?

It became clear that the *Gray Freighter* wasn't particularly spaceworthy. More of a training vehicle. I was a trainee, of some sort.

There was that to discover.

The engine room was a misnomer, imagine that. It was mostly an empty room. "Shepherds provide the interaction between anarchy *and* panoply," one of my teachers once told me. I finally understood what she meant. Rooms changed properties during wherespace. And Drexley was right—things could get weird in the engine room. A wire birdcage was on the floor, as if forgotten there by ornithologists. Its small hinged door was open. The three who came with me weren't talking, but I at least was included in that silence. I wanted inclusion. Lund wiped his nose, which made him look a lot younger than he probably was. America was out of breath, pressed her reddening hands to her face. "Hello?" Zenith called out, expecting an echo, receiving none. Everyone had done something sardonic and/or intriguing in the engine room, all except me.

Then I realized they were staring at me. The air was hot and thick and I wasn't sure if it was from the wherespace leaking in or from everyone's eyes on me. A point right below my collarbone started to tingle.

"What?" I said.

America leaned toward me by a few millimeters. There was a hairline crack in the air above me, and a shimmering hem of purple, and I knew that was from the wherespace or the shepherd, which meant that the air was literally hotter simply from their staring, and that was a pretty interesting trick of time and space.

"Can I, I mean we, see your, um, parts?" America was quiet and all vulnerable sounding, but with a suddenness of a door being thrown open, perhaps never to be closed again.

"Parts?" I said. Inklings of their talk-context floated inside of me, but not to be grasped.

"How do you say it?" Lund said. "Look, you're intersex, right?"

That word, said in front of my face with great infrequency in my life, was formulated even less in my own head. I started laughing, trying not to make it sound harsh—it was hard to know how these newfound peers would misinterpret.

"What?" America said.

"You want to see them?" I said. Guidance counselors from Li Po—I mean, from my hive on Li Po—told me that, yes, people would find my ilk strange, perhaps a little lewd.

Well, tough, I said at the time, but sex rarely came up at the Chartering, as I kept my distance from pretty much everyone. Except with Kathy, of course, and I did desire him—or at least I did before I stepped on the *Gray Freighter*. But even he didn't ask me too many questions about "the parts" in our lunch study sessions and fencing lessons. Now, as he was lost in shepherd-thought, guiding the ship, did he even see me at all?

These three were scrying me, that was for sure. America's bare shoulders had a damp glisten on them. "Don't be embarrassed," she said in a whisper.

"I'm not. Maybe . . ." I trailed off and turned my head to the empty bird cage, which was a metaphor provided by Kathy's shepherd to show how the ship's propulsion worked. It was the shepherd's totem. Maybe I expected it to have a bird, but then I thought that an empty bird cage was probably a better metaphor for me. "Maybe it's strange that I don't think I'm strange."

"You're not strange," Lund said, and I realized that all three of them—and probably Drexley too—were scared, and lonely, and not really glamorous at all. Except for perhaps a small, inner glamor, and anyway, we all had that. They wanted me to be the comet streaking across their vision, giving them a portent of something inside of them. I knew this. It didn't upset me. It only made me wonder whether these people could have been comets for something inside of me, or whether they were actually inert, and lackluster at the core, and tricking me.

Somehow, the patterns of our breaths were all matching.

Then the ship rocked and for a half-blink, everything inverted. The space between us shrank to millimeters, expanded to kilometers, and then resumed some semblance of normality. Whatever "normal" was in wherespace. Although everyone looked a little dazed, no one said anything about it. So I didn't either. And besides, it happened right before the good parts.

What was a little cosmic flux, right?

"Well," I said, gathering myself again, "I tell you what. Why don't we switch clothes? Why don't I wear what you're wearing, Zenith?"

"Me?" Zenith said, hand to her heart, and why was a fetching girl like that acting demure all of the sudden?

"You and you and you. All of you. Why not? Switch off. Here you can wear my dress, Lund. It seems like a fair trade. And you can stare at me all you want when I'm changing, I guess."

America shrugged and raised an eyebrow at me. Halfway between the phrase "I guess," she was already taking off her tunic top and tossing it to me, her whole infrared body glistening. I smiled and peeled off my gossamer dress and chucked my sandals toward Lund. Clothes started flying everywhere off bodies, and arcing across the engine room. Zenith unhooked her belt from the tips of her hair. Her heavy black clothes could have stopped fragmentation bullets; they were like something from a Panoptikon agent's battle wardrobe. It smelled like her skin. When I slipped and strapped them on, the inner shell warmed and melted and conformed to my body.

"You look pretty mean," Zenith said, laughing, but not unkindly.

The wherespace was in the room like incense. In some ways, the space-time continuum acted like a drug, releasing the inhibited from our chains of shyness.

In a minute we were all changed up. Breathless, I realized it was possible that they had never seen each other naked before in unison, that they were shier than I was about flesh.

A strange thought.

A stranger thought: I wasn't really aroused by any of this.

Still stranger: they didn't seem to be either. This, then, must have been truly novel for them, this role reversal and this restraint. I stopped worrying about whether they liked me or not and took in the slow pulse of the moment.

They were just clothes, after all.

We looked at each other. Lund had his hands crossed at his stomach. My opalescent silk dress reached to his mid-thigh. Glimmering tattoos of mythological beasts—unicorns, hippogriffs, extinct orcas—pranced up and down both of his legs.

"Cute tattoos," I said. He blushed but smiled.

Everyone was then sitting on the floor, leaning against the walls, careful not to jostle the birdcage. "Where did you grow up?" Lund asked me.

"Li Po," I said. "In the City of the Sextant." I had brief visions of home: my family of forty renting a swan pond for the day, the vendors who sold cinnamon gelato (God, how I craved gelato at that moment!) along the cross-hatched boulevards, the earnest prime schoolteachers who didn't know what to do with me.

"Were you born . . . this way?"

"Yeah, my parents are intersexed too. It's a colony of them. I mean, us." Detachment from my upbringing.

Zenith Marie's body was turning indigo. Perhaps she was imagining my family as being a continual circus. I could have assured her there was nothing that unusual about us.

Then, just as I was going to ask them about their lives, because I was dying to, Kathy strode into the room with a hurt look on his face and a limp, with Drexley a few steps behind. Zenith's body cooled a few shades.

"What do you think my girl wants?" Kathy started shouting, voice cracking, tears streaming down his face. The shepherd must have still been crammed in his head. He hopped on one foot, sashaying his disheveled dress, trying to put on a show. But he was in pain, from something I couldn't see. I assumed, at first, it was a "shepherd thing."

"Girl?" he incanted. Everyone was silent. "Girl?"

He clutched his head, tried to seem playful. His words slurred. It scared me. He really didn't know how he sounded. Twirling, he was desperate for notice and not given notice because of the desperation itself.

Hello, Kathy, I know you're in there, I wanted to scream at him. I know it.

The birdcage appeared to be larger, though I could have been imagining it.

Drexley also ignored Kathy, though he turned away with an almost tusk-like sneer. "What's going on?" he said. His face was beaded with sweat. "Why the hell are you wearing each other's clothes?"

"We're going on," Lund said, a little defiant, crossing his legs "and why don't you relax and stay awhile, Drex?"

"No way. I want all of you to robe and go." His eyes grew colder. "Robe and go!" And then he looked at me for an instant, his eyes searing me. The three others did stand up, and I did reluctantly as well. Kathy continued prancing as everyone remained motionless, almost hunched underneath Drexley's gaze. America found some gum from a tooth implant of hers and started chewing. She was beautiful. All of them were beautiful, each caught along the edges of their own quirks. I wanted to tell them that, as some way to commemorate that moment, but instead I decided to stand up and nod at Drexley's leering face. Everyone else kept their heads down, the moment gone. As Kathy sidewinded backward and forward, Drexley put a hand on his shoulder, clenched like a talon. He thought he had control of Kathy. And if he had control of Kathy he had control of the ship.

"What the hell are you looking at?" he asked me. He spat at the ground toward me.

The ship buckled again, and I snapped. When he started to turn away, certain in his subduing, I tackled him from behind. The dimensions of the engine room shifted. The birdcage that was behind us was in front of us. I could *feel* Kathy's shepherd in the room. It wasn't a pleasant feeling as we fell to the ground. I had caught his body totally off-guard, because he was woozy for a few seconds. Zenith's body armor increased in mass—maybe wearing such professional-grade gear had made her feel safer—and I knocked the wind out of him. The birdcage had quadrupled in size, and before Drexley could blink, he was inside the cage. I shut the door.

Everyone was speechless, except for Kathy, who screamed and ran back toward the bow of the ship.

I was breathing hard, doing my best not to run after Kathy.

"Let's go," I told everyone, "before he wakes up."

Everyone nodded, eying the cage.

———

I think a lot about how I came to the Chartering "rescued" because of latent telepathic ability. In some people's minds I was saved from a hovel of the intersexed! Elders at the Chartering kept telling me my cognitive scores were excellent, that it was not a problem that I had no shepherd yet, that some of the best telepaths in the history of the Parameter were tardy with their shepherd-bonding. As we ventured back to the bow, I thought for the first time that maybe a few of them internally linked my latency with the fact that I had a penis and a vagina. Which was ridiculous. But no more ridiculous than my peers giving horse names to shepherds.

I also believed that Zenith Marie and America and Lund didn't feel like they knew me until we traded our clothes, and this had nothing to do with telepathy—that awesome, frightening ability gave no connection. The only person on the *Gray Freighter* engaged with telepathy at the time, Kathy, was out of our orbit entirely. Thinking about those cruel orbits gave me headaches, and sucker-tackling Drexley didn't change the fact that I wanted telepathy with a shepherd of my own so very badly.

Drexley began shouting at us all to let him go shortly after he came to. I told my new friends—for we were friends, after what we had shared—that I thought Drexley was dangerous, and would hurt Kathy if he had the chance, and definitely me, and who knew who else on the ship. No one was safe. And I wanted to think that Kathy's shepherd, in that engine room, had *wanted* Drexley contained there, that in a primordial way it was trying to protect Kathy from whatever anguish Drexley had inflicted upon him.

We took turns to feed Drexley the gelato we scavenged, but he refused. He must have had an endo-hydration and food source that he had kept secret.

Explaining why I felt like I needed to keep Drexley locked up to the others took a while aboard the *Gray Freighter,* but hearing Kathy sobbing in his quarters was the real proof. I also laid out to the other three why naming shepherds things like Appaloosa and Jackie was chic yet astoundingly dumb. By the end, when we came out of wherespace after a couple of days, and a cordon of police rockets had surrounded our drop-point in the Blake system, they ended up agreeing with me.

And as the customs agents bound our hands and led us roughly to a holding ship, I wondered: would all of us move in the same spheres at the Chartering after this?

Still, when they booked us, we were all grinning. That had to count for something, right?

And that was that. It wasn't, however, quite as that-was-that as I thought it would be. There were a couple of other stories intertwined with this one, but none quite as important as my last story.

I could talk about the struggles of keeping Drexley hostage for two more godforsaken days in wherespace, until he finally, barely, settled down. I'd tried to talk with Kathy in wherespace, but he was distraught and trying to do his best to keep the wherespace journey intact, so I didn't want to bother him too much.

I could talk about my time in the prison at Zigurrat Station, charged with Commandeering a Parameter Vessel without Licensure. They put me in solitary and frisked me for state secrets and fed me split pea soup.

I could talk about how it finally happened: a shepherd coming to me in the middle of the night on my second day of prison, as I was sucking my supper from a gravy tube, and how my brain expanded sideways and elliptically. Just like they said. The shepherd gave its name (which shall remain nameless). I kept true to my word, and didn't give the shepherd a pet name of my own devising, or call it boy or girl. It was "just" a shepherd.

I could talk about how Chartering shocktroops rescued me from the jail (even though the jail was following strict Parameter penal code) and cleared my charges and whisked me back to the Chartering. There was no more precious commodity in the Parameter than people like me, and I needed care and constant attention during my first week of shepherd-bonding. It trumped everything, even Commandeering a Parameter Vessel without Licensure. When my prison guard gruffly protested, the black-vested Chartering officer (a part-time phys-ed teacher at the school) sighed and snapped the guard's pinky finger. I was able to eat lots of gelato at the Chartering upon my return.

I could talk about my year-long fling with America and Lund, but . . . no.

Now here's something. I could talk about how Drexley tried to shoot his head off with a zun gun. But they were able to reattach his mouth, and he's rehabbing on Mirabai very well, I've heard, so there's no happy ending there. His family ensures/insures that.

No, it has to do with Kathy. It's taken me a long time to realize that people are organisms, and are more mitochondrial than they want to believe. People bend, break, accrete with others in new forms. The rest of my time in the Chartering was uneventful in a good schoolgirlboy kind of way. I kept my nose to the screens, had a few, um, aforementioned affairs. But Kathy flat-out dropped out of the Chartering and disappeared after he was released from prison. I tried in vain to find any trace of him. Traces were supposedly easy to follow in the Parameter, but not his. He was gone in all senses of the word, and though I was guilt-ridden about the disaster of our joyride, I'd been plunged into adjusting to my new life with my own shepherd, with everything inflected and charged and changed. Kathy felt like an odd footnote from my not too distant past.

This last story happened three days before graduating from the Chartering. I had obtained a residency aboard a medical trawler on a Mirabai-to-Earth route. Not lucrative but not shabby either, which fit me pretty well. I decided to trek off grounds by myself and head to the Flowering Ape, for old times' sake—

I couldn't believe it, but I was already starting to sound like an alum. The curfew avatar had been banned; a few months before, I'd led a petition to the regents regarding that quite vigorously.

The place was mostly empty, but the place was smaller in actuality than my memory had constructed it two years before. I had to use the toilet, as I was the owner of the Parameter's smallest bladder. As I moved to the toilet, and passed under a big statue of the arms-crossed ape, I saw Kathy. He looked like he needed someone to talk to, preferably someone with professional training. His beard was long and scraggly, his dress a taut snakeskin that made him look ratty. His face was smeared with makeup, a terrible loosestrife blend. I imagined him putting it on in front of a mirror, hands slipping, crying, trying again.

When I sidled next to him, and he looked up—not at me, only at my movements—I saw that he was Rended. An untouchable among telepaths.

His shepherd had left him.

It was rare, but not unheard of, for a person on the brink of dissolution to lose that bond with a shepherd. In a way, it was worse than dying. Telepathy required sharpness, openness, acumen—three traits Kathy didn't possess anymore, it seemed.

His head rose up. "Hey you," he said, mumbling. He didn't recognize me. He reeked of illegal ethers.

"Kathy. Hey. How . . . how you've been?"

His eyes focused for the first time—on me, on my white, gleaming jumpsuit and my white teeth and the white lock of hair I braided in on a whim. I was embarrassed at how well I was doing. "Just wonderful," he said, without much conviction. He reached for a vodka juicer and squeezed the nozzle into his mouth. For all intents and purposes, it looked like he was attacking a nipple. I wasn't helping, I know. I wasn't helping. I watched a desultory duo of kids—Chartering prospects, no doubt—take the pods up and down the air shaft. Li Po, that green-pink pearl, was in full incline from the viewport of the Flowering Ape.

It occurred to me that, when Kathy gazed up and beckoned me down from a pod two years ago, his life was ending. He didn't know that; how could anyone ever know the precise moment when things would start to go downhill? When finally realized, it was usually too late. People back home in the colony write me and think I have some great foresight or wisdom because I can communicate with a shepherd, but nothing could be farther from the truth. On that night two years before in the Ape, I wanted nothing more from Kathy than a quick, sloppy kiss in the corner and some friendly inclinations. Now, our lives had changed—what could he have possibly wanted from me? Except, perhaps, to tell me to get the hell out of his life, you've already done enough damage.

If his life waned from that moment on, mine waxed. My mind shot out for a few nanoseconds to my shepherd, who was languidly orbiting Li Po. There, there, shepherd. Good shepherd. I didn't want to imagine losing my shepherd.

After he slurped and set the bottle down, I asked him, "Kathy. I need to know. What went on when we were on the *Gray Freighter*? What happened between you and Drexley?"

His eyes welled up with moisture, and he grabbed my hand, turned it as white as my teeth. But he didn't say anything for a minute, until he finally whispered, "What was going through me? A lot of pain from Drexley. I wanted to call him Drex so badly. He told me—" He started to choke up, and gave each word a phlegmy inflection.

Kathy let go of my hands and buried his face in his own. The kids in the pods above us stared. Who was this emotive man in a dress, they probably wondered.

"He told me that I wasn't good enough to take us into wherespace. That my shepherd wasn't good enough. He tried to have his own shepherd take over. And I liked him. I wanted him to like me. But he kept harassing me. He told me that I was worthless, my shepherd was worthless. And now . . . it's true." He turned his head from me.

"Why didn't you tell anyone?" I whispered, trying to focus on the past instead of the present, because the present was too painful.

"I was too stressed just to keep the ship on-course. And besides I was worried that . . . that everyone would have turned on me, even you, because they liked Drexley more than me."

"No, Kathy, they all hated him. Sure they might have been scared to show it, but . . ."

I trailed off. I didn't know how much I could have offered to him. Kathy was my friend at one brief, hot point in my life, but what did that mean? Crudely, violently, I thought I had "solved" the problem by tackling Drexley. But Kathy was too ashamed—or too damaged—to confide in any of us. Then he blinked out of everyone's lives.

How clumsy of me, that I didn't figure out the hints of the confrontation myself—the fluctuations in the engine room, Kathy falling apart in front of my eyes, Drexley's erratic control mechanisms—and then do something about it besides attacking the perp.

"I thought I belonged," he said suddenly. "I thought I belonged with something better than myself."

I needed to compose myself, needed to be "strong" for his benefit. "Why didn't you report it when you got back to school?"

"Drexley's family filed a preemptive slander order against me. My words wouldn't have meant anything. The slander spiders would have eaten up all traces of me, so I didn't try." He gazed at me with a hopeless, feral look. So that was why I was never able to track him down—Drexley and his lawyers made sure that I couldn't. That no one could.

I took his hand. He was trembling. "Kathy, I am so sorry. I really, really am." My bladder was about to explode. Clear thought was becoming increasingly impossible, and Kathy needed clear thought. "Kathy, I need to use the toilet. But don't go anywhere, okay? Promise me? I'll be right back, and we can talk about this some more."

He weakly nodded and slumped over. A bad Mirabain song laced through the speaker ether, a popular song about loving and caring that never sounded more empty to me. "I'm here for you," I said in his ear, but softly, so only he could hear. I stroked his long, course hair, and got up.

Splashing cold water on my face after I urinated, trying to control my breathing, pure panic spread through my body. Maybe it was a telepath's intuition, who knew, but as I ran, and before Kathy's table was in sight, I knew it would be empty.

And it was. His vodka pouch was tipped over on the floor. The kids resumed their pod racing, laughing. He was gone, and I was sure I'd never see him again, and do you know what? I haven't.

I really haven't.

Bulle**Moonlight** Is

On the first day of spring, Dispatch awakens me with a case.

"This is a good one," she says.

"Okay," I say.

I head over to my desk and log in. Holland, my partner, is already on the scene. An apartment complex looks ready to fall over, the fifth story on fire.

"Where are we—Morocco?" I say.

"Dijon," Dispatch says. "Now, listen. The building's been secured. Two kids were shooting each other over a Game Boy they must have stolen. But the Game Boy was coated in this poison—or at least the buttons were—and when the first kid—"

"What are their names?" I ask. Holland is still groggy. He's coughing and his *proxy* is polishing a gun to cover him.

"Don't have those yet," Dispatch says. "Anyway, the first kid shoots the second kid in the head, and starts playing the Game Boy, but then he dies right away."

"Wow," I say. "Okay, bring the family over here."

"Has the building been eradicated?" Holland says to me.

"Do you mean evacuated?"

"Yeah. That's it."

But the family moves into the trailer on the scene and there's no time to answer him. My *proxy* arrives, huffing. He was woken up too, even though it's the middle of the afternoon where he is. "Sorry," he says. *PROXY* is written on his vest.

"It's okay," I say.

When the family comes, I go over the incident with them. Holland is bored. I wish he would pay attention more. Two proxies, two detectives, four screaming kids, a mourning mother, a father trying to hold it all in, a few uncles . . .

"Wait," I say to Dispatch. "Is this for the first shooting or the poisoning?"

"The poisoning," Dispatch says. "The CO doesn't care about the shooting. The locals are handling that, detective."

"Right," I say. I start asking them questions. Our proxies are shitty translators. They try French, and then Arabic. Nothing seems to be getting through to the family, but I can't tell whether it's the poor quality of the translation or recalcitrance.

My proxy says to me, "Okay, uh, I guess the kids stole it from this video store . . . they shoplifted it, and they tried to work out turns to play it, but . . ."

"And it was in their possession at all times?" I ask.

A pause to ask and answer the questions in a language that I don't understand. It's beyond me. I treat it like noise, like the cooling fan on my remote access station, the humming from the connection.

"Yes, so . . ." my proxy says, "I guess they didn't see anyone else that would have been able to apply the poison?"

"Let us make the conjectures," Holland says, "proxy."

"Holland, easy," I say. "Okay, thanks. So get them to shuttle the Game Boy over. I'm sending you my contact info now." I send him my card. Then the father rushes Holland's proxy, passing right through Holland. My proxy shoots the father in the kneecap. The family is screaming, and they try to rush out while hauling the father away, but the trailer door closes on them.

"Okay, well now," I say, trying, to an extent, to keep things under control.

"Shit," Holland says. "'Board them all up."

"We don't have enough kits," his proxy says. He pulls a shield off his back and pushes the family toward the back, while my proxy cuffs the father.

"Let's back up a bit," I say. Holland is in the Chicago office. I've never met him, but we go back two years, which is a long time in this line of work. A French gendarme in camouflage pops his head in the trailer.

"Get the fuck out of the trailer!" Holland shouts at the gendarme, waving his arms. But the proxies are busy; mine is pulling the father through the front of the trailer for processing, and Holland's is putting a mesh layer down, preventing the family from moving forward. I can hear jets screaming overhead. The gendarme takes a step inside but my proxy, thank God, shouts at him in French.

"Jesus," Holland says.

"Holland, let's process the father and let the family go."

He stares at me. We can see through each other. "No fucking way, Jackson. They're all co-conspirators, at this point. Aren't they?"

"The father, yes, but look . . . we need to get moving on the poisoning. We don't have time to deal with every little nuance, do we?" My proxy comes to stand next to me. He looks upset. I can tell he's Muslim, and that's fine, but something's visibly shaken him, some instinct that he can't explain.

"Fine," Holland says, fading out. "Whatever. I'm on break, anyway. Get the father 'boarded up," he barks to his proxy. So soon I'm alone with the two of them. The trailer back opens up, and the family spills out, all running as hard as they can back to the apartment building. Helicopters are hosing it down, but it's unclear whether they're putting out the fire or performing crowd control.

"What is it?" I ask my proxy. "Did the father say anything to you?"

My proxy shakes his head, and the other one punches him on the shoulder and they start arguing. Then the French gendarme comes back, pushing open the door and standing next to all of us. In fact he's standing right inside of me. Then he pulls a cord at his chest and there are a ton of screams. I'm out. I jolt out and I have an earbleed.

"Ah," I say, leaning back in my chair.

"We lost them," Dispatch says on the auxiliary channel.

"Really?" I say, jamming Kleenex into my ears. "Is that so?"

"Sorry," Dispatch says. "I'll call a medic."

"No, no, it's okay," I say. "I'm used to it. Thanks, though."

"So . . ." I can tell she's still monitoring the situation. "I guess they're all dead."

"It looks that way." I stand up. There are three other detectives in adjoining cloakrooms. I don't speak to any of them, though Dispatch does. We each have our own caseload, our own partners. Beyond these cloakrooms are other tunnels, with other departments, other common areas and other apartments. I happen to live on-site. Detectives' apartments are about as interesting as their investigations and it's pointless to pretend otherwise.

So I fix my ear, get my equipment checked, process about a dozen outsourced warrants, shoot off a quick email to my therapist about the suicide bombing as part of protocol, and take a nap. When I wake up, the Game Boy is in a baggie at my desk. There's a toxicology report, which I skim. Something to do about a contact poison that is only manufactured in Yemen. Dispatch calls in to tell me that the owner of the shop is in custody already, and awaits me. Holland is already there. Holland never sleeps.

"France again?" I say, as I log into my desk.

"Actually, she's been moved to Romania."

"So soon?" Romania, then. She's Canadian. Her name is Amanda. Holland is in the corner, staring at her, sucking on a tooth. The interrogation room has a remarkable view of a desert valley, shielded by the shadows of mountains. Is it safe? It's as safe as anywhere. I had a choice, once, to enter the field, to see places as they really are. But that would likely have involved dying of sarin in some tin caravanserai.

"Hey," I say to Holland.

"Our proxies are fucking late," he says.

"I can hear you," Amanda says.

"Shut up," Holland says, pointing a finger at her. "Shut the fuck up."

"What are you going to do to me? You're not really here." She leans back in her chair.

"No, but you're not either, really. I mean legally. You don't have shit."

"So you're from Canada, huh?" I say. Both she and Holland stare at me.

"Jesus, Jackson," Holland says. Then the proxies come. They're bored, tired, overweight. There are no Romanians left in Romania. So Americans had to be shipped in.

"Sorry," mine says. Proxies are always apologizing the world over. "We had to process her papers with the warden."

"Eh, leave that to an underling," Holland says.

"We're the underlings," his proxy says, crossing his arms.

I lean forward to Amanda, eager to end this. "Did you poison the Game Boy?" I say.

"I have no idea what you're talking about," she says. "It was a resell. Someone sold it to me like—"

"So what the fuck is a Canadian doing in the middle of fucking Dijon operating a secondhand video game store?" Holland says.

"I don't have to tell you," she says. "It's not important."

Holland sighs. "This is getting really old." Then he tells his proxy to hit her jaw with the back of his gun. After the proxy does that, Holland asks her again about her goings-on in France. She remains silent.

"Do you support the global Intifada?" I say.

"Who doesn't?" she says, straining against her chains to try to touch her bruised jaw. She's not attractive. Her brows are too bushy and her arms are too thin.

"I'm not going to answer that. Are you Muslim?"

She shakes her head. "I'm French Canadian."

"Well that explains something," I say, more for Holland's benefit. But he isn't buying it. My proxy is struggling to pay attention.

He looks tired. The warden comes in. Amanda is still defiant. She starts saying her name over and over again. The warden is a middle-aged woman with a tray of iced tea in plastic liter bottles.

"Everything going okay?" she says. She's the middle-manager type that one finds so frequently on the crumbling edges of Western civilization.

"Everything's fine," Holland says.

"That's great," she says. She smiles at us and sets the bottles down for all those actually present. The proxies relax and take the iced tea and drink up. After a few seconds, Amanda does too. Then she presses the bottle against her cheek, leaning her head forward, on account of the chains. The warden lets us know that if we need anything, we should contact her, she'll be in the garden. Then she leaves through a side door.

"So you didn't know those kids?" I say.

"I'm kind of glad they stole it," she says, coughing all of the sudden. "I mean, not that they died, but that . . . I represent . . . the enemy to them. Because I can't understand what they understand . . ." She drifts off. Then she tries to throw the bottle at my head, which upsets me. I thought she would have tried to bean Holland, since he is clearly the vicious, unrepentant asshole. But on second thought, she probably doesn't make a distinction between the two of us.

I tell my proxy to pick up the bottle, but he doesn't hear me.

"What?" he says. "The little guy is waiting to set sail. He's just waiting your instructions."

"What?" I say.

"Jesus fucking Christ," Holland says. He swipes at his own proxy. "Pick up the fucking bottle." But he's ignored. Amanda starts laughing, and it's contagious. Our proxies slump to the floor. I move to Amanda, move through the desk she's behind, and stare at her, an inch from her face. Her pupils are dilating and her bruised jaw is like a half of a plum.

"Did you poison that Game Boy?" I say. She reaches up and puts her hand through my face. I think she tries to cradle it, caress it?

"I'll talk to you again," she says. Then her head slumps down. The proxies are quiet on the ground also.

"Holland?" I say.

"I'm going to find the warden and find out what's going on," he says.

"Be careful," I say, on instinct.

"Jackson," he says, "we're not really here. Remember?"

"I guess."

"You know, it's strange," he says, not really listening to me, "I feel kind of bad about Amanda. I usually have good or bad feelings about people. My feeling about her was immediately bad— but maybe I was wrong." Holland manages a smile. "Just this one time."

"It takes a big man to admit mistakes," I say, without much emphasis. At that moment I want to be rid of him. And then he's gone, into the garden. I call Dispatch. "Our subject and proxies are down," I say. "They took some iced tea . . ."

"What?" she says. "Hang on . . ." There is a fly above Amanda. It lands in her hair. I lean back against the wall and for a few seconds I don't know where I am. I'm a trainee in the Academy. I'm a small boy running on a beach crowded with unlicensed beauticians and mechanics and driftglass. I'm burying my mother and taking my sister to school in our neighborhood shelter. I wonder whether my detection skills have held me in good stead.

"Jackson, you need to get out of there. You need to disengage."

"What? Listen . . . I'm going to check on Holland." Our projections have a range of about fifty meters.

"Jackson, no, listen to me—"

Then the connection jams. I open the door to the garden. It's enclosed with high white walls, and it's night out. I didn't expect night. There's a full moon and a cold wind. I imagine that it's cold. The garden is green grass about ankle high, wasted myrtles with blue flowers ringing the trunks, a swimming pool in the center. There are denser woods farther back. I can't see the end and I don't see Holland anywhere. I edge toward the pool. When I get closer, I see red mudpuppies skittering in the water. And beneath them, the body of the warden, face down on the bottom, weighed down with a brown belt. Her skin is greenish.

"Holland?" I call out. Maybe he's already disconnected. I'm out of my element. I hear a whistle and look up. The warden is there on the flat roof of the interrogation center. Or rather the false warden. She waves. She's placing what look like round, gray stones on the roof.

"Backup!" I yell. But there's no one to hear me. A gaunt little man, about two feet high, peeks over the edge of the roof and jumps off. He's naked. He starts running toward me, wielding a knife that's as long as his body. He bounds through the air in long leaps. I start running. I mean to find Holland. Never leave a partner behind. I learned that in the Academy. I edge around the pool and launch past trees and into the woods, startling geese—I have no idea what geese are doing in the woods—who push away with alabaster wings. The little man is swearing at me. I look up at the moon, and a monstrous cloud passes over its face.

Stumbling on a root, I feel him leaping onto my back, clinging to my neck. His body is slick with a light syrup and it's with a surprised pleasure that I can feel this, and smell hickory charcoal, and hear the little man's breath against my ear. That he is a ghost like me.

"I'm sorry," I tell him.

Then he's gone, and there are about five medics and security agents—I can't tell them apart—standing over me, prodding me, holding my wrists down. I see Dispatch's face on the edge of the circle. I shout at all of them and I'm detained and sedated.

I wake up and recover just in time for Holland's funeral. It's closed casket, since his real body was electrocuted and charred in Chicago beyond all recognition. I don't actually go to the funeral, but Dispatch sets up a special hookup, parking an interrogation unit outside the gates of the cemetery. The Plot of Detectives is surrounded on all sides by crowd-control bunkers and ivy inter-laced with barbed wire. Throughout the ceremony, I keep having images of the warden's body being defiled by her impersonator. She's just been dragged out of the pool and the impersonator assesses her body, then pulls down her soaking pants and I can't think of anything worse, I keep thinking. Then the father who we detained in Dijon, who was blown up, starts pissing on the two of them.

A color guard shoots off a salute with shoulder rockets. Bible verses are read, projections of doves released. Holland's family from Nova Carolina thought of that. Holland was never very religious. I've never considered before whether I actually like Holland until he's lowered to the ground. It wasn't that type of relationship. We'd worked well together on the beat. Few suspects liked us. Pretty much everyone we talked to was a suspect. Detained subjects become biologically alive but legally dead. The transformation is pretty simple, as easy as pointing a gun in someone's face.

Now I have to understand, by myself, what is in front of me. I'm off the case. I'm given leave. I don't want to leave. I return to my office environment and Dispatch is waiting for me.

"Do you want to get a coffee?" she says.

"Okay," I say. "Sure."

We walk through the quiet linoleum tunnels. "So the safe-house in Romania was destroyed," she says. "Firebombed. You're very lucky, Jackson."

"How . . . did Holland die?"

"The enemy's found a way to interact with detectives. So the whole program's being put on hold. Until my superiors can find countermeasures."

"Countermeasures." I don't know what that means for me, whether I'll have to be retrained or not.

"That's right. But it's not anything you'll have to worry about," she says.

"So how . . . how did I live then?" I ask.

"I overrode the blocking field and disconnected you. It was close." We pass functionaries in thirdhand suits, functionaries in innocence masks, functionaries pushing handcarts full of black boxes and freeze-packed hands. Occasional skylights reveal the sun, far overhead.

"What about the case? The Game Boy? The assassin."

She stops and puts a hand on my shoulder. "All those things don't matter anymore. They were probably, I don't know, going to use the Game Boy to assassinate someone? That seems likely, doesn't it? Or maybe someone pawned off the Game Boy on Amanda without knowing any of this." We reach the Starbucks set in a common area atrium. I order tea for both of us. At the table, she plunges into her life story. She tells it with urgency, as if she might never see me again. She grew up in Pensacola . . . her parents were from Nicaragua . . . 2nd team all-state in field hockey, but there weren't a lot of field hockey teams in Florida, so it wasn't as big of a deal as it sounded . . . lost everything . . . developed throat cancer after a dirty bomb but beat the odds . . . runs a podcast on world music in her spare time . . . a few other memory-based knick-knacks . . . For the longest time, she has been just a voice to me. When she finishes, I take her hand, even though this is against policy.

"We're going to be fine," I say. "Aren't we?"

She sips her tea. I watch her hands.

"Your partner, Holland," she says. "You know, he was never very nice to me. Does it make me bad to think that? To dwell on his flaws? What do his flaws mean to me, anymore?"

I tell her that Holland's flaws still live with me, that his carelessness got him killed. I don't tell her about the thoughts I have when my eyes are open.

"I'm going to recommend you as a consultant to my superiors, while you recover. Listen, Jackson, when the time comes I want you to tell them everything. Spare nothing. Because they'll want to know everything. They'll be asking you a lot of questions."

"What kinds of questions?" I ask.

She wraps the tea bag string around her finger and squeezes out ochre drops.

"We don't know yet," she says. "We don't know where yet. A safe place, of course, where you can consult . . . for a while. Consider it a lateral career move."

"So you're telling me to pack for a long trip?" I ask.

She puts a hand on my shoulder. I almost expect it to pass through. "Take care, Jackson. I have to go to headquarters. It's a long trip to Nome."

As she stands up, I stand up too. "What about the garden? Was it destroyed too?"

She shakes her head, as if I've confirmed a theory she's had about me, that her internal inquiry has come to a successful resolution. "Garden? There was no garden there. We don't have a budget for gardens. It's a wasteland there, remember?"

I take my tea and smile at her. I have indeed realized my foolishness. "I remember," I say. I take a sip. Then she's gone. A man with no arms cleans my table. His Starbucks apron is streaked with red juices. The rag is in his mouth as he bends down and wipes down. He has an array of lapel pins, indicating campaigns, on his apron: TAJIKISTAN, BHUTAN, HORN OF AFRICA NIGHT RESCUE. I put a Liberty Gold chit in his side pocket and he nods and smiles. I wonder if my efforts have served to protect him.

And I don't forget his face as I walk back to my quarters. It's easy enough to log in again—Dispatch had left the last location in the system, and I've observed enough over the last few years to find my place. I arrive where I last was. The detainment center is rubble and empty. The moon is monotone. Shadows cast a black and white world. A sprinkler jettisons water droplets on the lawn. I take off my shoes and socks. I peer at the sprinkler as I pass it. It's not water coming out; it's a coppery liquid. I bend down to the grass and run my hand across it, then lick my palm. Acrid and smoky. I get on my hands and knees and lap up the water.

"I'm here with you," Amanda says. She puts a hand on my neck and strokes it. "I'll make sure you won't take too much. Just a controlled dose."

"Right, but it killed you," I say between sips. The water is pesky and it's hard to get a lot of it into my mouth. But I get enough.

"We're not in that world anymore."

"Which world is this, then?" I feel both lucky and guilty that I get to ask some follow-up questions.

"The one that I was trying to pretend I didn't know existed. The one that I was killed for, because I knew about it."

I stumble to my feet toward the swimming pool. I've always tried to operate within the strictures of the laws given to me, which I admit have cast a pretty wide net.

Doing otherwise was never part of my employment profile.

On the other hand, I'm unemployed now.

The warden's body isn't in the swimming pool anymore. But there's a long knife floating on the surface, like a leaf. I bend down and pluck it out. My hand takes to it. There is a straight-and-narrow trough, about a hand's width, that I haven't noticed before. Azure tiles run along its sides. There are three other troughs, and they all divide the backyard into quadrants. Mudpuppies of rust stare at me as I walk past. Their eyes are white.

The sprinkler stops. It's done its share to wet the grass. I want to cry about how peaceful the night is. I'm walking on the grass blades toward the woods. My strides grow longer. There really isn't any way to explain this. I put the knife between my teeth and sail forward through the air. One of the little men meets me in mid-flight and tries to get a handhold on my body. I move my body sideways, as if I have no depth at all.

"The jinn come from the mudpuppies!" Amanda calls out from below me, cupping her hands. The bruises on her face are gone. Then she says something in French. Her homeland is gone. "I mean, the mudpuppies are incubators for the jinn. The people who made this world try to control them. But . . . they have minds of their own."

"Got it," I call down to her. The jinn lands, and leaps back toward me. "I should have taken your condition more seriously," I say to her as I land and pivot.

"Ah, well . . ." she says. Then she jumps up toward me and embraces my body. I worry that she's going to drag me down, but she doesn't. "I wasn't honest," she says. "Those kids died because of me. I knew someone was going to try to steal the Game Boy, so I poisoned the start button. Then I just . . . panicked, and gave it away to these two kids who were milling about."

"Why . . . why was it so important to begin with?"

"It's not the Game Boy itself. It's the game cartridge that was in it. The Saudis had a covert program, where they wanted to upload suicide bombers to a virtual paradise. They were to present this as a 'gift' to Hamas—but when Hezbollah and Hamas started attacking each other . . ." I feel her shoulders twitch. Time can slow for any reason. "The Saudis abandoned it. Anyway, it's the same technology that lets you become a ghost. Except, with this game . . . it has a neural link, see? And people equipped with the right link themselves can access this place at any time. This game was the prototype for mass production. But then I stole it. And things got out of control."

"You weren't in a great spot to begin with," I say. I see, behind me, the jinn spring through the air. He has a black blade hoisted in both of his hands above his head. "Who was trying to kill you, Amanda?"

Amanda closes her eyes. "God is behind everything," she says, letting go of me and settling back to earth, "and yet has no capability to alter our circumstances. Having that capability—to be inside of us through even the smallest manifestation—would destroy everything we hold dear." She wipes her nose with her sleeve. "At least that's what I've heard."

"I really couldn't say," I say, as I jump upward, arcing the knife in front of me. The knives clang and mine rattles down, slicing the shoulder of the jinn. He screams and plummets.

"But things didn't go as they planned, exactly. I mean, I'm dead, but I'm here. And the jinn keep hatching. No one really controls it anymore. People are trying to control it, but . . . It's not really God's fault that I'm dead," Amanda says. "Whose fucking fault is that?"

"I don't know, our Coalition of Interested Forces? Me?"

"Well, you know, your government resuscitated the garden. It was a cultural exchange program with the Saudis when they started training Christian suicide bombers alongside the Sunni ones. I swear, Jackson, one day this is all going to be washed away."

"Like my guilt?" I say. Because I'm beginning to feel guilty.

"Well," she says, "let's not get carried away."

Knowing that, I want to comfort the jinn, but he is gone, and his blood trail is lost in the slick grass. I slide to the ground and take toward the woods, following the water trough. I don't look back to Amanda for anything. I still don't know who she works for—or worked for—and what she intends to do, now that she is stuck in the garden that she wanted to destroy. The trees in the woods are slender, spaced in measured proportion, and the grass thins. Feathery conifers. There is an angular trail.

I see, farther off through the trees, the gendarme who blew himself up—though he really wasn't a gendarme—shoot a kid in the face.

"Hey!" I say, running toward them, winding through trees. "Hey!" The kid falls back and drops the Game Boy. When I get closer I see that the other boy is also on the ground, twitching, poisoned. The gendarme moves to pick up the Game Boy, paying me no mind. Because I am still far away, I throw my knife at his hand, which slices it off. He doesn't scream—why should he?—but instead throws his gun at me. The gun slices off my right hand.

"You know," I say, feeling nothing except an itch inside my other hand, "that is really not fair." I pick up my hand off the forest floor and after stuffing it into my pocket, pick up the gun. When I reach the cop, he is hunched over the Game Boy, trying to balance it against his knee and start it up.

"There's no game in there," the shot boy says, sitting up. A gosling sleeps in his caved-in skull. "I threw it over the roof."

The cop shushes him. "Do you mind? I'm trying to get this thing to work."

"Into the water treatment pool," the boy continues. "There are a lot of fish that live in there. I was hoping one of them would eat it. And then one of them did!"

At this the cop closes the Game Boy and looks at the boy. "Who ate it?" His severed hand lunges toward my face, but my own hand flies out of my pocket and meets it in mid-air. They spar, fingernails clicking.

"A white carp, big as me!"

Then the cop lunges at the kid, but the other kid wraps his arms around the cop's legs. He falls over.

"Who do you work for?" the kid says, pounding his fists against the cop's back. "Who do you work for?"

I pluck the Game Boy from the ground and keep walking. From the stump of my severed hand grows a clutch of blue peonies. The stems tickle. I move in further. There are geese sleeping underneath the trees, but I don't want to disturb them. I walk for about ten minutes or so until I reach the wall. It's too high to climb. The trough ends at the wall at a little groove, where the water trickles to the other side. I crouch down and try to see what's there, but no luck. I put my good hand into the water and try to feel where the water goes, but I'm only able to squeeze three fingers in. Then I feel someone else's hand on the other side. We fumble around for a second in the cold water and then we both retract. I press against the wall and listen, and hear breathing.

He makes the first move, though, the first recognition. "Jackson?" he says.

"Holland? Oh my God, where are you? Are you all right?" I say.

"Yeah, I'm all right. Really." His voice is on the faint side.

"Uh, where are you again?" I ask.

"Right next to you. Just a little farther out. In the desert."

"Right." I want to figure out what to say to him. There were so many times we found ourselves in war zones, trying to inflict

policy on strangers. We never had the chance to test our partnership. And now that partnership is over.

"I can't talk long . . ." he says.

"So . . . how are you?"

"Oh, pretty good," he says. "I've been wandering the desert a
lot. Writing poetry."

"Poetry?"

"Sure. Do you want to hear one? It's short."

"Okay," I say, studying my flowered hand.

The heart's falcon flutters over the blotter
A forced battle does not crown a victor
Innocent amusements are found wanting
The sparrow glides in terror

"I like it," I say. "I don't know too much about poetry, though,
I have to admit."

"It's a struggle," he says. "But thanks."

I want to bring us back to the matters at hand, before they
completely slip away from us. "They're going to torture me, Holland. When I wake up. They're going to send me to Nome and
interrogate me about the garden—"

"Yeah, about that . . . Here, take this." He lets go of my hand
and pushes a game cartridge through the watered slot. I pick it up.
The plastic is fog gray and it's a bit heavier than what I would have
expected. There's a small pearl eyelet mounted on the wider edge
of the cartridge.

"It's wet."

"Doesn't matter. It'll still play. You have the Game Boy, right?"

"Yeah. Where . . . where did you get this?"

"I got it from the mouth of great trouble. But, listen, don't play
the game until you're ready. Okay? Promise me that?"

"I promise."

"You sure? You might not be able to go back."

"I said I promised, Holland. Jesus."

And this, at least, gets a laugh from him. "Okay. Okay. Do you remember how we were recruited, back in the day?"

"A little."

"We were failures at the police academy, Jackson. I mean, we were at different academies, but same difference. Why were we chosen to be ghosts?"

"Because we were bullies and horrible detectives who thought we were great detectives," I say.

"Okay. Close enough. We never really detected anything, did we?"

"Not really. But how about now?"

"It might be a little too late for that. I have to go now."

I know I'm never going to speak to him again. "Holland! I can jump to the other side!"

"You can't."

I'm not even sure if I want to. But I put the cartridge in my coat pocket and try to leap up over it. It doesn't look that high. I go about twenty, then thirty feet up, and the wall's edge is just beyond reach.

"I told you," Holland says after I land, trying to catch my breath. "It's okay. You're not ready to go outside the garden. Look, just watch what you see, and you'll be all right."

"Watch what I see," I say, with disbelief, as if the conversation is finally catching up to me. But then he's gone.

I lean up against the wall again and hear birds rustling and chirping on the other side. I close my eyes. When I open them, I see a little paper boat coming toward me in the trough, from the direction of the swimming pool. The jinn is inside. I move out of the way of the miniature canal. His arm isn't as badly damaged as I thought it would have been. I smell ginger and incense. His paper boat has a stiff sail, but when he gets closer to the grooved opening in the wall, he scurries to collapse and lower the mast. As he passes, we look at each other, but I can't tell, for the life of me, what he's thinking. He manages to lower the sail in the nick of time and then, so he doesn't get decapitated going under the notch in the trough—which is rather low—he lays down in his boat and crosses his arms on his chest, like a vampire leaving paradise.

I then realize that the cartridge that Holland has given me will not be there when I wake up. Nor the Game Boy.

Because they are not real.

The moon is so bright. It's not asking a thing of me. I put the cartridge in the Game Boy and press START. I sit and wait against the stone wall for about a month. Frogs sit in my lap and lumber away. Geese land on my shoulders and sleep, and depart again. Bees pollinate my peonies, and die, and the descendants of those bees come back to the hand. I'm waiting for the moon to turn new, to vanish. When it does, and I can't see anything, not even a single flower in front of my face, I have a conversion. In the darkness I'm shot through with a joy that I don't deserve.

But as to what I'm converting to, that will always remain a mystery.

# of AThe Wildfires

I loaned *Roxy: Shark * Flower* to the Antarctica Institute
for the Arts because I wanted a better life for her; at the same time,
it soon became apparent that the same problems that vexed me in
regards to her behavior would trouble the museum. Although she
was out of my hands I still carried an interest in her well-being, as
well as an aesthetic sense of pride, and an interest in whether her
time in the museum would appreciate her value.

Was it punitive on my part? I suppose it was. But she was the
one who threw everything away. *Roxy* once had everything she
ever wanted: protection from thieves, food.

There are many others like her in the museum—though no
two alike; that indeed could be a journeyman's definition of art—
and I was assured there would be opportunities for supervised
interactions with other objets d'art with her same level of genetic
provenance. And no expense would be spared in her preservation.
Her display case contained the ambient full-spectrum lights that
she needed for the chrysanthemums and poppies and amaranths to
grow along the seams of her arms. *Roxy* would not be able to harm
herself or others with her serrated molars, since they were capped;
when they shed, the cap would grow with the new tooth. (The
museum and I agreed to a 50/50 split on residuals for the aftermar-
ket sale for the teeth no longer in her mouth, for the scrimshaw of
majestic oaks the artist had encoded there.) A daily spore spritz-
and-dry would keep her hair—coarse on her crown and spine,
ultra-fine on her arms and legs—from losing its luminous sheen.

And of course the museum gave me the opportunity to watch her every hour of the day. The surveillance bees would always be with her. I was a busy man, but I rarely left the villa, so I often checked on *Roxy* throughout my day. It soothed my soul.

Here is *Roxy* sleeping, curled up in a ball in the corner of her case, the bees bobbing around her head.

Here is *Roxy* eating a block of nutrience, then another.

Here is *Roxy* in the greenhouse yard—named the Van Gogh Arboretum—with a soothing panorama of the Dutch countryside circa 1900 all around her. The museum, of course, is in West Antarctica, and the Dutch countryside is underwater, but *Roxy* has no way to know of these affairs. She hangs from her tail from one of the oak trees (a predisposition on her part that the artist cleverly integrated into her DNA) and swings gently, watching everything. There are only five or six other pieces of the collection allowed in the greenhouse at the same time. I certainly have interest in seeing what else is being accomplished in the field, and by whom. Two particular pieces catch my eye: Mareanxerias' *The Epoxy Disaster of Late Model Capitalism* (a hairless golden bear cub with horse quarters) and *Paint! Paint! Paint!* (a taxidermied wolf head attached to a cherry-colored, wheelless motorcycle chassis and eight spidery legs) by the sublime master Ya Li.

Epoxy and *Paint* always stand next to each other, and rarely exercise or relax. Their legs twitch. At first I think it is a glitch but after a museum guard attempts to separate the two, I realize that they are communicating to each other. The two shuffle apart before the guard can reach them but slowly gravitate back together after his departure. This occurs over the course of several days during their hour-long stays in the Van Gogh Arboretum.

Roxy begins to find this curious. She has never been willing to make the first move with anything, but one time she presses her body against the glass of the panorama, close to *Epoxy* and *Paint*. As if trying to capture the false sunlight in her body. (She does not photosynthesize.) Eventually *Epoxy* and *Paint* look over at her in unison, and soon the two in conversation-by-tapping become three, though I have no way to know how *Roxy* has picked up on such a vernacular, since she was never taught such things in my villa.

Still, this is worrisome. I alert my concierge at the museum and soon enough several guards come into the Arboretum to put a stop to this extraneous socialization. They are heavily armed with nonlethal coercive wands. *Roxy* sees them approach and her nostrils flare. I try to connect to my concierge again to warn the museum staff but before that can happen, *Roxy* wraps her tail around one of the guard's necks and snaps it.

Roxy tries to dash away, but nano-netting swoops down from the ceiling.

Even *Epoxy* and *Paint* seem scandalized. They try to disentangle themselves from the melee, but are caught in the netting as well.

Roxy's access to the Arboretum is revoked, and a guard is in sight of her display case at all times. I should feel horrified and disappointed, but I am not. Because I know that *Roxy's* errant behavior is deep-seated and incapable of being cured. I once tried instilling discipline into *Roxy* by telling her which rooms she could and couldn't enter in the villa. The kitchen: only when it was time for her to eat. The foyer: only when guests were present for a reception and she was beckoned to remain motionless there. The study: never, under any circumstances. The library: never. My wife's rooms: never.

But she never listened.

The next day I send an invitation to *Roxy's* artist for a light afternoon lunch at the villa and a leisurely suborbital artillery firing. He agrees. I can tell he is reluctant.

Artists are a necessary evil in my world.

John Priestly—such an old-fashioned name—flies in from New Yellowknife. His skin has a bluish sheen to it, and I can't tell whether that is from a side effect from his latest anti-aging treatments or preparation for using his own body as a genetic canvas yet again. Perhaps they are the same thing.

On the rooftop overlooking the burning hills, we sit down for lunch and I ask him about a possible restoration job of *Roxy*. One, would this be feasible with a minimum of cost overruns, and two, would this decrease her resale value at auction?

He sips his tea and stares at me for a long time. "*Roxy: Shark * Flower*," he says at last, "is far more perfect than you can ever imagine. I wouldn't dream of altering her, not a single strand of code."

I smile and recount her latest exhibition of aberrant behavior, perhaps laying the blame for her disposition at his feet. After all, I have always believed the artist has a certain moral responsibility for the very act of creation.

John leans forward and pierces a grape with his fingernail. He draws the grape to his mouth, as if he is a poison-tester. "Each piece of art is unique, and has a different effect upon each person who encounters the work. Would you have asked Goya to make *Saturn Devouring His Son* a little less violent? Perhaps, you know, 'tone it down'?"

I tell him, this time without a smile, that I paid 500 million for *Roxy*, and that he's no Goya.

He laughs. "No, no I am not. No one is, anymore. Not even Ya Li."

I stare at him, and tell him that maintaining his artistic integrity is all well and good, but that *Roxy* is slowly becoming a menace, if she is not one already.

"And how do you not know that this, too, is part of what makes her beautiful?" He shakes his head, and speaks to himself, as if I had suddenly disappeared, and he was left alone in a stranger's house. "I once thought like you did. I worked so hard on my craft, and to make sure that people like you remained pleased. But now . . . no." He is sure of his rightness, and I find this frightening.

I stand up, and he follows suit, and shuffles to his helicopter without a farewell. It turns out that we will not be shooting satellite armaments into the ruins of Buenos Aires—together, at least. I discount his outburst as mere petulance. He loves his helicopters and studio-fortress and fame too much. He will never change.

After a week of constant confinement, *Roxy* appears to have calmed, though her behavior is a bit erratic. She paces, she sleeps, she makes tiny trilling noises from the back of her throat. She tips her head back and laughs. I have never seen her laugh before. A troupe of teenagers from New Dubai traipse through the museum halls, disinterested in any of the work, soldiering on as if polar explorers from another century. As they walk past *Roxy*—the tour guide wisely decides not to dwell on her—she splays herself on the glass of her case and bares her teeth, her double line of fangs.

All of her teeth are uncapped.

Several of them begin shrieking, placing calls to their parents and nannies to rescue them. The tour guide fumbles with the emergency response interface attached to her arm. A sleeping gas fills the case and fogs it. *Roxy* struggles and lashes out, longer than I thought would have been possible, until at last she slumbers. She is taken to the Department of Restoration.

The next morning I decide then that I need to buy some new art to clear my head. A fresh start for my collection.

As I make preparations to fly to Cape Adare—my favorite gallery spot—I wonder how *Roxy* will respond to restoration. John Priestly would have been the ideal candidate for the task, of course, but that is out of the question. The museum has the best team on the continent. So they say. I hear that *Epoxy* and *Paint* are in restoration as well. The atmosphere has been growing more chaotic in the Arboretum, even with *Roxy's* absence: more scuffles with guards, more cunning attempts at communication with other pieces of art.

In a way I am already beginning to say good-bye to *Roxy*, as a squandered investment to write off. It will hurt, but not as much as these constant tantrums on her part. Art, above everything else, is a sign of one's station in life, and it is difficult to properly display one's station if there is not decorum.

I am about to put on my favorite art-buying suit and go up to the helipad, but I get a ping from the museum.

Roxy has escaped.

My body trembles. I desperately want to harangue the museum concierge, but instead I hang up and retreat to my study. I turn on the camera view of *Roxy* and breathe a sigh of relief: the surveillance bees are still active.

I see cacophony. An alarm has gone off and *Roxy* is running, alongside a galloping *Paint* and *Epoxy*, past display case after display case. Many are opened and empty. A museum guard stands in front of them, sparks flying off his gloves. *Paint* leaps forward in an arc and punctures the guard's heart with one of his legs. *Roxy* fumbles through the guard's red uniform, and rips the interface patch off his arm, and puts it between her teeth.

They keep running. *Roxy* thinks she is going to make it. She thinks she's going to be safe—though she's still terrified, even I can sense that. More guards behind them—they hesitate. Those three works of art are worth more than a thousand of the guards' lifetime salaries combined. In that second, *Epoxy* puts a hand on *Roxy's* shoulder, and pushes her in another direction, away from the oncoming crush. She runs into a colder, narrower tunnel, and affords herself only one look back. The look is anguished. The halogens affixed in the ceiling grow dimmer, and then it's almost dark, and she stops.

The bees have kept up, and they start to luminesce. She scowls at them. The link is still there. I can't imagine what I would do without that lifeline. She puts her hands on her knees and catches her breath in the near-dark. It must be a service tunnel she is in, for museum employees.

She hears screams and shouts, and considers going back. But she takes a few steps, and there is dim light ahead. She starts walking forward again, her hand on the wall, which is jagged and powdery.

The air's ventilation is thin here. The tunnel curves left, then right. She is determined, which is clear from the look on her face, in her hunched shoulders and tense tail.

When the light grows bright enough to see by, she takes her hand off the wall and starts running again to the end of the tunnel. There must be lag; the bees struggle to keep up and I see the back of her ragged shirt as she runs.

The end of the tunnel is a rock wall with a porthole set into it.

She presses her face against the window. She sees a hangar on the other side. A huge space, as large as my villa, with a ceiling that can't be seen. About a dozen large-scale art installations are in the hangar—massive, bulbous. The airlock to the arid outdoors is closed. The largest installations float, and *The Leviathan* is the largest of them all—three blue whales conjoined at the head and attached to a hovercraft, looking like the floating petals of a gargantuan poppy flower. On their sides are embedded the complete works of Jackson Pollock. The artist, a native to the continent named Tin Hester, was funded by the Antarctic Arts Research Council to buy the paintings on the cheap, since Pollock really hasn't been in favor for quite some time.

It is magnificent.

About a dozen people in gray suits work in the hangar—jetting near the larger installations and hovering like dragonflies to tweak a propulsion unit or diagnose an adhesion rivet.

Roxy crosses her arms and tries to decide what to do next. They will find her; she is sure of that.

No—I see it in her eyes. She is trying to figure out how to do what she already plans to do.

This is the moment that should be flagged, sent higher up the food chain, when a predator is neither contained with other predators nor immediately threatened.

Roxy says something, but I can't understand it. She bangs on the window, and then takes the guard's interface out of her mouth. She presses a few buttons on it and casts it aside. Then she retrieves something else from her mouth, from underneath her long tongue. She slaps a small patch of yellow goo on the window and she takes a few steps back. I'm told that they've finally made a connection with her again. They are coming for her.

She covers her face. The door blows open. Metal shards nick her, but she manages to sidestep most of it. There's a yellowish fog in the corridor; the goo keeps emitting smoke. Behind her, guards call for her. She calls back, but again I can't understand what she's saying.

She darts into the hangar, choking but staggering forward. I can't see her because of the mist. The guards plunge through the broken doorway as well, but they are not prepared for the mist, and they halt and begin coughing.

I cannot see *Roxy* in the hangar at all, but in another minute, the hangar door heaves open, letting in the bright, unyielding Antarctic sunlight and the dry, bitter air.

The art installations' cables have snapped; whether it's because of the mist, I cannot say. I am shaking. They slowly float out of the hangar: a hot air-balloon attached to a large black heron, a hybrid of a dragon and a biplane. *The Leviathan* is the last to leave, as the whales' bodies rotate slowly. *Roxy* is still nowhere to be seen.

That's when my bees start to die. The view of the hangar gets fainter and scratchier, and then there is only the blank screen the color of black pearl.

I feel feverish. I stand up and check on my wife, who is resting in the study. I see—if only for an instant—*Roxy*'s face in hers. That is why it is important to understand art before you buy it, to know how to see what is in front of you. But after my wife entered her coma, I became not only a connoisseur, but a patron. Commissioning *Roxy* with my wife's DNA was not theoretically legal, even in Antarctica. But I would not be deterred.

I stroke my wife's gray locks of hair. She doesn't stir. I feel the breath from her breathing apparatus. When *Roxy* broke into the study—what did she know? How could she have known of my wife?—she must have stared at my wife's face and seen something of herself there, some unblemished vision, without the animal splicings, without the flowers blossoming inside her arms.

That's when she tried to unplug my wife. I found her just in time. She shrieked at me in babble—of course it was incomprehensible—and darted past me. I called the local militia and explained the situation as I struggled to keep up with her roaming through the villa. I should have known that *Roxy* was veering toward my wife's old suites. She managed to break in and lock the main door behind her. When the militia finally entered the locked-off suites by cutting a hole in the ceiling, *Roxy* was dressed in my wife's favorite peacock dress and had torn all of her favorite paintings off the walls—Degas, Twombly, Hals—and stacked them in a pile. My wife has always been old-fashioned; she cared little for contemporary art.

Roxy was also wielding, with her tail, a broadsword from my wife's extensive medieval armor collection. The first fool who dropped through the ceiling was beheaded with surprising force. Blood gushed everywhere, but *Roxy* was careful to put herself in front of the paintings, so that they wouldn't get spoiled. It took a dozen militia soldiers to stun and subdue *Roxy*.

That was when I decided she needed to be loaned out. I immediately sold all of the paintings that she had torn off the wall. I could not bear to have them within my villa.

Roxy would have ruined everything with my wife. Yet I am upset that she is gone, and likely dead, because she didn't give me the chance to ruin her.

I exit the study and put on my suit and then go outside. There is a smog advisory around Ross Bay. Along the shore, the hills of bell heather and the crabgrass burn, only a few kilometers from the villa. No one is going to stop it from burning. There's no point. The weeds will grow again and burn again. The air has a pink tinge; I actually think it's beautiful.

If *The Leviathan* were to come to me, I would not see it descend, until it was almost too late. What would my wife have thought of those Jackson Pollocks? Surely she would have been riveted by the sight?

I go back inside. I try to put the incident behind me. Cashing the insurance settlement helps. Many of the works from the museum are recovered—albeit damaged—but not *Roxy*. I decide that I want to go shopping in earnest this time, for a work of art that, by active contemplation of it, will help ease my unease. I put out feelers for a few weeks to the best galleries.

I cross John Priestly off my list, naturally.

After a week, when I am ready to visit my favorite galleries in person to bargain for a sale, I receive a package, about half my height. It doesn't list a sender. I am often the recipient of enticements from galleries. After the courier leaves, I take it to my study—it is not heavy at all—and press my hands against the black box. The sides flop open.

Inside the package is a sculpture of me. Though only a meter tall, it is like me in every aspect. Its skin gleams white as mine gleams. Its eyes are opalesque like mine. Its hands are at its sides. I am filled with both flattery and fear; flattery at the daring attempt at hyperrealism, and fear from the blank, unnerving stare from my miniature twin.

It is staring at me. Its head has moved imperceptibly, but it now looks in my eyes. I am transfixed, despite my best efforts. I immediately desire to know who the artist is, and what the genetic provenance is. As I take a step toward it, the sculpture turns its head to one side. It's like a glitch, or as if the sculpture is thinking or listening to an inner voice.

Then the objet d'art puts both hands against its ears, squeezes tightly, and rips its own head off.

As the sculpture holds its head aloft, I manage to glance over at my wife as yellow mist spews from its neck.

Tyrannia (II)

This is the story of people.

This is the story of other-people.

This is the story of other-people who roamed the land and hunted people in the caves and tunnels where the people had retreated.

This is the story of the other-people's collections of plucked wings and talons, which they wore.

This is the story of those who took sides.

This is the story of those who didn't take sides.

This is the story of the rumbling of the other-people as they swept across the meadows, spiky garlands on their shoulders.

This is the story of wind-swept thistles.

This is the story of the people's one and the other-people's other-one, who found concord after many trials.

This is the story of the wide sky, and the birds that would spread their wings, but would be unable to fly.

This is the story of what people would mark on the cave walls, and the other-people would cross out, sometimes with their own blood.

This is the story of the one, who the people said would never amount to anything.

This is the story of the one venturing out of the caves alone to hunt and stare at the unbutchered clouds.

This is the story of the shapes of clouds resembling animals.

This is the story of the snare that the one set, hoping for hare.

This is the story of the one's snare catching a surprised other-person by the foot.

This is the story of the dangling other-person who was also known as the other-one.

This is the story of the other-one's banishment to the meadows and woods of the people.

This is the story of the one looking down at the other-one and shaking her head.

This is the story of the other-one's stubborn prayers as he lay trapped.

This is the story of the golden mushrooms that grew in common shafts, nurtured by both people and other-people.

This is the story of the news river, which wound from cave to cave like a thirsty serpent in the territory of the people.

This is the story of the other-one tracing the scars on his face after he was loosened by the one.

This is the story of the other-one's scars.

This is the story of the long stories told on the walls by the people and the other-people, the sun shown on the walls, the battles and triumphs and failures against the giant birds, for those stories were common between them.

This is the story of the valley where the people would have their visions of the dead who have not yet died.

This is the story of thistles puncturing necks.

This is the story of the other-people offering skeletons of the people in crypts far below the earth, to gods that they couldn't name.

This is the story of bloody vapors coursing through the tunnels.

This is the story of the other-one looking up at the golden sky and trying to decide how to get home.

This is the story of the other-one, after being freed, trying to decide whether he wanted to go home.

This is the story of the other-people proclaiming that the other-one must be captured, and that any who harbor the other-one would be destroyed.

This is the story of quicksilver bubbling in a brook.

This is the story of the other-people clicking their plucked talons together, and listening to the wind for the footfalls of the one and the other-one.

This is the story of the one expecting no quarter from the people.

This is the story of how the other-people would dream of giant birds plucking their eyes and limbs.

This is the story of how the people would dream of docile giant birds who would come to them in friendship and not enmity.

This is the story of an empty site, a valley where the people would skin and eat bears and leave the bones for vultures.

This is the story of the beetles biding their time in the tunnels of bloody vapor.

This is the story of the other-people fanning out across the meadow and hearing the other-one's hissing snores.

This is the story of the other-one's dream of scar creation.

This is the story of three nameless people depicted on an obelisk that came before the people and the other-people, their faces crossed out as a warning.

This is the story of the one hearing the other-people sprinting toward them in silence.

This is the story of running.

This is the story of bears ambling further up the mountain.

This is the story of breathing.

This is the story of not breathing.

This is the story of the cliff above the site.

This is the story of the other-one taking the one's hand and, upon reaching the cliff, leaping forward.

This is the story of the fall.

This is the story of prayers by the other-one as they fell, doused in paints extracted from the golden mushrooms, trying to get all the prayers they could.

This is the story of the other-one dressing the one's leg.

This is the story of the one thinking that she was having a waking dream while the other-one sang to her leg, imagining his head as that of a bear's.

This is the story of malice.

This is the story of how the two couldn't speak to each other, since they shared no language between them.

This is the story of rain-swept towers dreamed outside of the caves in shadows and meadows.

This is the story of minute differences between people and other-people.

This is the story of the other-people coming down the tenuous footpath and capturing the other-one, and leaving the one for dead.

This is the story of quiet prayers by the one, because the one didn't want to appear too bold or angry in supplication.

This is the story of what is not learned by gathering words.

This is the story of a cindered stick against the cheek and the desire to know something.

This is the story of a time when rescues and redemptions were possible.

This is the story of the other-one wondering what kind of trouble he had gotten into.

This is the story of the one's prayers being answered.

This is the story of the bird with antlers.

This is the story of the bird with antlers wondering how it received antlers.

This is the story of the clouds above opening up into a map of lightning.

This is the story of the long journey to a cage.

This is the story of the deep isolation that the one and other-one shared with each other, across much distance.

This is the story of the bird with antlers indicating that the one should mount its back.

This is the story of the other-people asking questions of the other-one inside the pit.

This is the story of the bird with antlers darting across the meadows, gliding in short hops.

This is the story of the bird with antlers following the map of lightning.

This is the story of the other-one not saying a word as to its change of heart.

This is the story of tiny white flowers blossoming from the seams of the scars.

This is the story of the other-one imagining wrapping his arms around the one's waist.

This is the story of the silence that wasn't meek.

This is the story of the maw of the arterial cave that the bird with antlers approached.

This is the story of the other-one dreaming of flightless birds within the pit.

This is the story of the night-eaters wondering among themselves what it must be like to have a body.

This is the story of the bird with antlers scurrying away from the cave, leaving the one at the entrance.

This is the story of the cave walls, lined with stories of skeletons.

This is the story of the past in the future and the future in the past.

This is the story of the long-sloping tunnels populated by beetles.

This is the story of the skeletons embedded in the cave walls and arranged in the outlines of winged bears.

This is the story of the other-one hearing the echoes of footsteps.

This is the story of the signs that the beetles gave to the one and the other-one to follow them.

This is the story of the one knowing nothing of the other-one's scars and memories.

This is the story of the days within the tunnels by the one, and then the lost memories of what constituted a day.

This is the story of how the prayer-receivers do not appear in stories, only the shadows of stories.

This is the story of the darkness in the tunnels, and the one following the pincer-clicks of the beetles.

This is the story of the mutual consent of clouds and night.

This is the story of the secret stronghold deep under the earth that the other-people had captured the other-one within.

This is the story of the thousands of gold mushrooms giving light in the massive cavern.

This is the story of the apparent emptiness of this cavern, except for the beetles, and their cousins, the father beetles, who hung from the ceiling.

This is the story of the dwelling in the center of the cavern, made out of wood.

This is the story of the one entering the dwelling of wood, though she was afraid.

This is the story of the light from the golden mushrooms casting shadows upon the face of the one.

This is the story of the pit in the center of the dwelling.

This is the story of the other-one in the pit, without teeth.

This is the story of the other-people guarding the cage with their talons and thistles.

This is the story of the one afraid.

This is the story of the one stepping inside her fear and finding herself there.

This is the story of unspoken memories of malice finding a home inside the one.

This is the story of laceration and poison finding home inside the one.

This is the story of sharp stone and heavy stone finding a home inside the one.

This is the story of cold air and bound hands finding a home inside the one.

This is the story of shouted questions and whispered questions finding a home inside the one.

This is the story of the other-ones watching the one with dismay.

This is the story of friendship.

This is the story of the one screaming.

This is the story of the other-people lancing the one with thistled clubs.

This is the story of the other-people puncturing the one with spears.

This is the story of the beetles growing angry.

This is the story of the other-people entering the cage and beating the other-one with thistled clubs.

This is the story of the other-people pushing their spears into the body of the other-one.

This is the story of a gray bird flying out of the one's mouth and a white bird flying out of the other-one's mouth.

This is the story of birds flying.

This is the story of the other-people who spent the rest of their lives alone, though they were together, thinking they were right.

This is the story of the people who kept away from the other-people's pain, and were also alone.

This is the story of the two birds flying up the tunnel, to the light.

This is the story of the birds' tools: their beaks and talons, which would never be stolen from them.

This is the story of how they learned to love each other.

This is the story of the white bird and the gray bird eating both sadness and joy, now that they were both together.

This is the story of the house of wood and its pit laying in wait for the shifting of the earth, and the cracking open of caves.

This is the story of the people and other-people one day coming together, so that they both died and lived together.

This is the story of the one wondering how she had wasted so much of her life before she turned into a bird, staring at clouds.

This is the story of the other-one becoming friends with the beetles, and flying toward the fallen bodies.

This is the story of the birds flying.
This is the story of the birds flying for us when we fall.
This is the story of our scars.
This is the story of clouds passing over our scars.
This is our story.

The Philip Sidney Game

Several years ago, I started writing a story about a man who was flying into Minneapolis-St. Paul and saw a car crash from above. The plane was about a thousand feet up and was descending when he saw the crash. It was late at night, a red-eye flight, so he could only see the headlights and taillights, and the faintest silhouettes of the cars. One car began to swerve and careened into the opposite lane, grazing the driver's side of an oncoming car, which halted. The car that caused the accident stalled for a bit but then accelerated again and kept moving forward. While the hit car was motionless on the road, another car from behind slammed into the back of it, pushing it off the side over a small embankment that the passenger could barely discern. Then that car jerked backward and kept driving as well.

The road this took place on was just an ordinary road connecting one suburb to another. There were a few buildings—warehouses, maybe—close to where the crash took place, which were unlit. And a pond in the back of one of them, weakly shimmering. This was what the passenger saw, terrified. The plane continued its landing and made a swooping turn toward the airport, flying away from the scene.

The passenger, buckled in, clenched the arms of his seat. No one else seemed to notice the accident. Everyone on the plane was quiet, sleepy. Then the landing gear went down and soon the plane was on the ground.

This was where I had left the story for a few years (twelve, actually): The man stepping out of the jetway and into the airport, which was still crowded with travelers though it was very late at night. I got busy with other things, other stories that seemed more important to finish. I had left the passenger hanging there for quite a while, in a daze on solid ground. His life was sketchy. In fact I had no idea why he was flying to Minneapolis-St. Paul in the first place. Whether it was the beginning of his journey or the end, or whether he was only trying to make a connection, I couldn't say.

In a way—if one really thought about it—this suspension wasn't really fair to him, or the mystery that unfolded a thousand feet below him. Or I guess to the people in the accident. I pretty much forgot about the story fragment, and looking back I'm not sure why that was the case. Maybe something about the story scared me.

But I had found it again when cleaning up some old files on floppy disks. Scavenging the disks for any useful scraps before I recycled them. I actually had to go on eBay to find an external disk drive that would read the damn things. Most of the files were either documents I had transferred over to my MacBook already, or were pieces of ephemera like grocery lists or addresses to fiction magazines, or whatever. What caught my eye about the story of the car crash, though—before I had even read what the fragment was about—was the file's name: "the_philip_sidney_game." I didn't ever remember calling it that, and in fact after reading the file couldn't begin to think what connection the title would have to that story. I knew Philip Sidney was a poet around the time of Queen Elizabeth, but I was embarrassed that I knew almost none of his work, or what he had to do with a game. I asked my wife Kristin but she had no idea either.

After transferring over the file, I did my best to pick up the thread of the story. I wanted to see where I could take the passenger after he landed. But it wasn't easy. I had the passenger moving through the airport in a daze, through the Gold Concourse, down to Baggage Claim. (Actually, since I had begun the story twelve years ago, the concourses in the airport were renamed after letters instead of colors. I stuck with the colors.) The passenger retrieved his one blue suitcase and then took a shuttle to the rental car lot. Still shaken from what he saw from above, he tried to consume himself in mundane tasks like showing his driver's license and credit card to the counter agent at the rental car company. Soon enough he was on the road with a map-brochure in his lap. After about ten minutes he was in front of the business-class hotel that was allotted to him for his trip. The unassuming hotel was in one of the outer suburbs, next to a highway junction and the corporate headquarters that he was supposed to be visiting. The next morning, in the hotel's computer room, he scoured the Internet for any sign of the accident on any local newspapers' websites, but nothing was to be found. He began to wonder whether he was imagining the entire thing.

It was beginning to annoy me that the story was set twelve years in the past—I couldn't give him Wi-Fi. At the same time, I felt that I had to be true to the original intent of the story, which I had yet to discover. I was a very different person twelve years ago, more prone to needless pyrotechnics. Back then, I was also much more likely to pepper a story with self-referential and oblique cues to let the reader know *at all costs* that he or she was reading a story and not to get too comfortable in the story's illusion. It was fine, as far as it went—a necessary albeit coy stage in my growth as a writer, I guess—but this time I didn't want to do that, at all.

Anyway, the passenger gave his presentation in a beige-colored conference room and during his lunch hour he decided to go hunting for the scene of the accident. He didn't know the Twin Cities at all, so he didn't have his bearings to where the crash would have happened in relation to the airport. What was more, it was raining. Cold for early May, or colder than he was used to. He tried to imagine any feature of the road or the buildings that were at all familiar. Or the pond—but he knew that the area had hundreds of bodies of water. He first drove on the highway. But soon he took an exit and found himself on less congested roads. Every intersection looked like every other intersection, with an equally dispersed amount of gas stations, fast food restaurants, nail salons, and the like. And in between those clusters, houses. Not too large and not too small. Not too opulent and not too desolate. He took roads that wound around knolls, and these gave him hope, because he knew that the second car in the accident—the one that had received the most damage—tipped into an embankment. But nothing looked familiar to him at all.

After a few hours of this, his cell phone rang. Apparently his clients in the suburban headquarters had called his superior back in the home office, because they didn't have his number. They were upset at his absence. Before much could be said, he turned the phone off.

It was starting to get dark. And the rain wasn't letting up. At this point in the story, I hadn't decided whether the passenger was going to find anything or not, any clues about the accident. Or perhaps the accident didn't happen at all. As the twilight closed upon the passenger, I paused and tried to understand just what he wanted in the first place. It wasn't really clear to me, this obsession of his. I worried that if I left this matter unsettled, he might be in his rental car for another twelve years before I figured out what should be done.

So with this impasse, I didn't write anything with this story for a few weeks, and was in danger of losing the thread again. My interest in any particular project always waned or (less frequently) waxed in ways that I never understood. The desire to start something would take over me, but then it always came down to a matter of endurance. I was always impatient, always looking for the next batch of kindling to set on fire until the smoke became thick and redolent, and there were more embers than flames, at which point I would almost always step away, scouring for fresh fuel. It was slash-and-burn agriculture of the mind. Every once in a while I'd circle back and blow on the embers, throw on a few more sticks, and start the cycle over again.

Oftentimes, this was the best I could hope for.

As it turned out, I had my hand forced on this issue when I received a package in the mail. The package had heavy brown wrapping and many three- and five-cent stamps that looked somewhat faded. My address was typed on a mailing label. It had a Minneapolis postmark but no return address. I opened the package and found that inside there was a bubble-wrap lining and a floppy disk. There was no letter or other note in the package and no label on the disk. I was worried about my computer getting infected from the disk, but I decided to take a chance. I couldn't have very well thrown it away. As the disk whirred in the disk drive, I saw on my desktop that the disk contained three files, named A, B, and C. I checked the properties on each one, but there wasn't any information about an author. The only possible clue was the file creation date, which was in early May twelve years ago. The date the files were "last modified" was the same. I took a deep breath and opened the first file.

The story picked up where I had left it—not where I had left it a few weeks before, but twelve years ago, with the passenger landing in the airport. I thought about calling the police but the idea upon an instant's reflection seemed absurd. All I could do was read; no matter how anxious this made me, I could do little else.

In this continuation of the story, the passenger immediately took the car out to search the roads for the site of the accident after he landed. He just drove—all night, relentlessly, without stopping, through serpentine suburban roads that he couldn't name. When dawn was about to come, with faint gray light filling the sky, he found what he was looking for. He pulled over along the side of the closest warehouse, in a weed-strewn parking lot. He got out of his car and looked for any sign of the cars, or the accident.

Nothing was conclusive. He saw skid marks leading off the road, and shards of red and white plastic, and glass. The sun was beginning to come up. Not sure of what he would find, he walked around the warehouse on the western side of the road, finding no signage on the building except for a letter "A" in a white stencil, about the size of his hand, where a doorbell would normally have been. He even tried the lone door, but it was locked. He did the same with the warehouse on the eastern side of the road, which was identical to the other warehouse except for the letter "B" in the identical place.

He went back into his car and tried to decide what to do next. Then he heard a noise that he first thought was from his car. He turned off the ignition, but the sound kept getting louder. It was above him. He rolled down his window and looked out. High above was a silver propeller plane, like an outdated commuter airliner. From the clouds above that plane came another plane, a black jet, in a tailspin. The propeller plane didn't evade the second—or didn't seem to know it was even there—as the black plane grazed the tail with its nose and continued downward. There was a screeching sound. A devolutionary was making its sacrifice. (Those were the exact words of the story: "A devolutionary was making its sacrifice." Which made little if any sense to me.) The black jet, in its chaotic descent, managed to right itself and arc upward, though still wobbly. The passenger looked in dismay, however, as the silver plane spun around as if drunk. As it fell, the passenger closed his eyes because he knew, at that point, that a third plane would slam into the silver plane and he didn't want to see that at all. He stuck his head back in and rolled up the window. After a few seconds, with the tornadoes of broken engines getting louder, he heard the debris falling all around him—crashing into the warehouses, in the pond, burning fuel in the damp grass, fragments of planes raining on the road itself.

The passenger was unharmed. The story ended.

After reading this, I stared at the screen for a long while, trying to decipher, in a figurative sense, what I had just read. I worried whether this was some kind of cryptic terrorist threat, an extrapolation from my half-story into the realm of real-life action. However, I had no proof this was the case. I probably wasn't helping matters by spinning out the worst case scenarios of bodily harm. It could very well have been a prank or an elaborate ruse, though I couldn't understand how the beginning of my story could have been available to anyone. I had found the original disk, with many others, buried at the bottom of a desk drawer, unused in over a decade.

On the other hand, the story's ending was such a spectacularly ridiculous idea that I had to give it credit on a storytelling level. The prose was clear; a little plain, but certainly not a disaster. It didn't *have* to be the end of the world that someone was completing one of my stories.

Then I remembered that there were two more files on the disk.

I avoided reading them for days. I made excuses, and tried to work on "real" writing projects. But I wasn't able to make any progress on any of them. The thought of completing my own version of the passenger's story made me nauseous. Not at least until the mystery had been resolved, or went away, though I had faint hope for the latter.

To bide my time, in a way so that I could deceive myself that I was actually being productive, I Googled "the Philip Sidney Game." I first thought, before I knew any better, that it was a more-or-less random phrase, one that had no connection to the story at hand as far as I could see. What I found out only complicated matters; I shouldn't have been surprised about that.

The Philip Sidney Game was a theory of evolutionary selection. There was a legend that, when the knight-poet was being carried to safety away from the battlefield after being shot in the leg, he asked for a water. But then he saw a soldier—a common foot-soldier at that—look at his water bottle with excruciating thirst. And Sidney said: "Thy need is greater than mine," and gave him the water bottle.

Sidney died twenty-four days later. The story never said what happened to the soldier who received the water. And although I had a hard time believing the reality of this situation, the fiction of his martyrdom outweighed what was undoubtedly a gruesome death from a bullet in the thigh. He was a courtier, a favorite of Queen Elizabeth, and an altruistic soul.

Moving away from the realm of fanciful yet empathetic anecdote to that of game theory—the dying soldier needed some way to signal that he was thirsty to someone who had water. This required an expenditure of energy. Everything would have to come at a cost.

But what if there were three dying soldiers around poor Philip Sidney, and they all cried out for water? And moreover, the act of crying out put them all in such a poor state that, if they didn't receive water, each would die. All things being equal in this case, the signals canceled each other out. Sidney would have been unable to find out whose the greatest need was.

It took me a while to realize that this thought experiment had, in the eyes and minds of behavioral scientists, nothing to do with his poetry. And the more I read about the game, the more bewildered I became. There wasn't anything in either my story or the continuation that seemed to have anything to do with the dictation of need from one person to another. The passenger was alone.

At last, restless from the stalling, I asked Kristin if she would read the remaining files for me. I often had a problem reading an email or letter that I knew would contain bad or unpleasant news, which I tried to avoid more often than not. She knew this about me and said she was waiting for me to ask her. But she would only do that for the second file—I would have to buck up with the third. I agreed. It was a Saturday morning when she started reading the second file. I took a walk around the neighborhood with the dogs—it was a May day that felt like July. When I came back, I asked her whether she had finished the second file and she said yes and that I wouldn't like it. But she also thought it was best for me to read it myself and make up my own mind.

I stalled for another hour or so, the panic rising, but I ended up sitting down and reading it, scanning it once and then forcing myself to read it more thoroughly.

In this continuation of the story, the passenger retrieved his luggage, picked up a rental car and drove to his hotel—a sequence the same as my own recounting in all but cosmetic differences (which made me shudder). The next morning he gave his presentation and returned to the hotel.

From there, the passenger took a different path. He didn't go out of his way at all to find out what happened with the crash or to confirm that it even happened. He just did things, performed tasks. He ate lunch, went back to corporate headquarters to lead a follow-up Q&A session regarding his presentation—which was very well-received—and then had dinner with several of his clients in the hotel restaurant, a steakhouse with a steak that was a bit too tough. He was satisfied by the day, although there were several times when he had to push down qualms about not trying to find anything about the accident. But he managed to quash guilt effectively, and concentrate on the matters at hand: steak, purchase orders, shots of Jaeger, and baseball.

At this point, I let my guard down a bit. I was expecting something far worse than a mere twist in the tale. I told this to Kristin and she told me to keep reading. She was beginning to look upset herself.

I kept reading. The passenger, now tipsy, stumbled to the elevator and to his hotel room. It was good he wasn't driving; he thought briefly of the accident again, that maybe the driver who had triggered the awful chain of events was drunk on a dark road. When he was lying on his bed, trying to think of nothing, a manila envelope was slipped under the door. The passenger sat up, and then ran toward the door. Opening it, he looked both ways in the carpeted corridor. No one was there. The envelope was unmarked. He sat at his desk and opened it up. Inside the bubble-wrapped interior was a text-heavy document printed out on dot-matrix paper. The paper smelled like the spray used in bowling alley shoes. The passenger began reading the text, which was a story called "The Philip Sidney Game" by Alan DeNiro.

I scraped my chair back and stared at the story from a middle distance, as if moving a few feet away from that page would cause my name to transmutate into someone else's, or disappear altogether. Kristin grabbed my hand, and said that the story wasn't done. I moved closer to the screen, though not as close as I had been before, and kept reading.

The passenger read with dismay, and then with terror, about his plane ride, his descent into the Twin Cities, his witnessing of the accident, his ensconcement in the minutiae of his business meetings. And while he read, he wondered just who this writer was who had known so much about him. Since there were many pages, he skipped ahead to the end of the voluminous story, in which he found that he, in this particular story, was locked inside a cavernous warehouse. There was also a grievously ill horse in the warehouse with him (though it wasn't clear what the nature of the sickness was), which was pacing the warehouse floor but did not panic. There were also loud bells clanging in a slow 4/4 time, and blue spotlights that turned off and on in time with the bells, and satin drapes that floated through the warehouse of their own accord.

This character's reading habits were extremely disappointing for me, needless to say, because the passenger was impatient and only interested in the big finish of his story, and had no inclination to find out what mysterious forces had led him to that end. No matter what would end up happening, those gaps would disturb me. And it was as if the author of this story knew this.

The passenger then took the local phone book out of the hotel room's desk drawer, and started looking for my name. That was how the second story ended.

I put my laptop on hibernate, and then turned off my cell phone. It was an instinct that took hold of me. I wasn't sure about what to think about the disk anymore, and the stories on it. I tried to convince myself that they were just stories, and bore no real meaning to my everyday reality. After all, if someone had gone to the trouble to send me this disk in the first place, they must have at some point uncovered my name. In the perverted logic of what had already taken place, this story within a story in which I was a character was perfectly normal.

Of course, I went to bed that night with no feelings of normalcy. As I drifted into sleep, I hoped that in the morning I would have a clearer sense of what should be done.

I didn't remember dreaming that night, but had a sense after I woke up that I had been put through the ringer. I couldn't trust what I couldn't remember. My suspicions were confirmed when Kristin told me that I was mumbling something about "devolutionaries" as I slept. I would often have night terrors that I would never remember. Although the severity of them had lessened after I started taking anti-anxiety medication, every so often I would sit up in bed and try to push away some monster (such as a vicious dog, or crocodile) that I thought was in the covers with me. Or I'd wake up on the verge of drowning, clutching my throat.

Devolutionaries, then. Exasperated, and not feeling rested at all, I took it upon myself to take a walk with the dogs in the early morning light. Kristin was already at work. I needed to clear my head and think about the genesis of the matter: where I was in my life when I had first written the story fragment. To retrace and exhaust every possible step.

As I walked with the dogs through the neighborhood, I ruminated about my life twelve years ago. I had just moved to Minnesota from Virginia to be with Kristin. I was still trying to find my way around the Twin Cities. It occurred to me then that I had begun this story thinking of my own descent into the Twin Cities for the first time, on my first visit, a few months before I had driven up with all the belongings I could fit in a Toyota Corolla. Did I actually witness a car crash from above? I had no memory of such a thing. I had just started writing the premise in my notebook . . .

The notebook. I had transcribed the story from my longhand scribbles into my computer originally.

alan deniro's tyrannia

When I got back, I tore through my old closet. I had saved all of my all notebooks since college, all of them, even though I rarely looked at them. I was afraid to throw away what might have been considered a part of me. I scoured through the various cheap, spiral notebooks I had at that time in my life until I found the story. Flipping through the pages, I was brought back to that time in the story's creation: my first bitterly cold winter in years, holed up in a city I didn't know at all, aching for spring. The story fragment had indeed started in the exact place as the computer document I had originally created.

It didn't end there, however.

At the end, when the passenger stepped off the plane into the airport, still shaken up from what he saw, he received a call on his cell phone. He didn't recognize the number. He answered it.

The line was full of static. Then a low voice on the other end told him that the devolutionaries were watching him, and he was not to recite The Words, warning him not to be a fool. Then he hung up.

That was how I wrote it. The Words.

I might not have thought this ending worth transcribing, a dead end, too cloying and conspiratorial. I had no idea what I was thinking with the *devolutionaries*. Who were they? Did I really write that? It seemed so. I couldn't help thinking that this warning was meant for me instead of the passenger.

Then I poured myself a bourbon on the rocks and sipped it as I sat at my desk, Googling and bookmarking everything I could find on Philip Sidney, to try to immerse myself in the world of this story. I felt like I had a bomb of metal fragments sitting at my desk, and that the only instructions to diffuse it without tearing me to shreds were encrypted in a PhD dissertation on Elizabethan literature. I did in fact try to cull what I could from centuries-old books that were digitally scanned and online. But I wasn't finding anything that threaded the needle between my original story, the files on the disk I received, and the

bridging section that I had orphaned in the notebook. Nothing
fit all of this.

I went to his poetry:

For me, alas! I am full resolved
Those bands, alas! shall not be dissolved;
Nor break my word, though reward come late;
Nor fail my faith in my failing fate;
Nor change in change, though change change my state . . .

I went to his "Apology for Poesy," his manifesto (before there
were manifestos) on how poetry's value came from the interplay
of moral teaching and heavenly delight. Then I Googled "Philip
Sidney" and "devolutionaries" together, which I should have done
long before. There was the usual Internet detritus of nonsensical
spam pages that crammed together both words along with thousands of other randomly generated ones. *Philip Sidney cologne for
elk $199.99—free shipping, viagara are you feeling your urges devo-
lutionaries?* But on the second page of results, I found a page called
"Philip Sidney and the Secret Societys of Aeropagus," which contained a poorly scanned monograph from 1839 in JPEG format on
a Belgian server. My hands were trembling as I clicked to the page
and started reading the monograph by James Rosemount-Ettiene.
In the monograph, James claimed that one of Sidney's secret
diplomatic missions on the continent, when he was governor of
Flushing in the Netherlands, was to form a secret society called
Aeropagus. Acropagus I had heard of, albeit only in my recent
Googling—a rumoured literary society that included Sidney,
Edmund Spenser, Sidney's boyhood friends and poets-in-arms
Edward Dyer and Gabriel Harvey, and a few other minor figures.
The goal of the Aeropagus (one of them, at least) was to "clas-
sicize" English verse by using Greek and Roman syllabic forms,
rather than Anglo-Saxon and Norman rhyming schemes. It was
thought in this circle of poets that this form of verse hearkened
back to a purer, almost priestly form of poetry, in which the Greek

and Romans used verse accompanied with music to predict the future, proclaim terrible truths, and so on.

However, the concrete existence of Aeropagus had been disputed for centuries—many scholars have thought that Spenser's one reference to Aeropagus in his correspondence was meant to be a joke. And at any rate, this form of verse was only one of Sidney's interests; he wrote plenty with "conventional" rhyme and meter, cribbing at will from Italian sonnet forms, for example.

In this monograph, though, James claimed that there was *another* Aeropagus, a secret society within the secret society. There was always a mystical bent to Sidney and the poets in his circle; after all, one of Sidney's mentors was John Dee, the notorious English magus and favorite of Queen Elizabeth who regularly asserted that he could summon angels. But this inner circle of Aeropagus was a commission by Queen Elizabeth herself, to establish a beachhead of "scientifick philosophy" on the continent. In the guise of a diplomat and governor, Sidney could gather onto him all of the arcane learnings that were flourishing on the mainland of Europe, particularly in Holland, Italy, and the German principalities. In this way, Sidney could fine-tune the metaphysics of poetry, in the manner of incantations, in order to fully utilize knowledge of voice, rhetoric, and musical diction to (piously, of course) access the conduits of heavenly wisdom for magical aims.

This was the passage where James had mentioned the "devolutionaries":

"Sir Philip Sidney had found no small measure of success in his experiments in vatic verse—that purely by metrical speech and on occasion musical accompaniment, a poet could not only speak to the future, but also enter a state of terrible apprehension and, through chant, 'project' oneself, theosophically, into past events, and even into the thoughts of others, with physical distance being no impediment whatsoever."

I read that again, and once more, and tried to wrestle with what James was proposing, or whether he was even being serious.

But I had to trust that he, at least, believed it—or if the connection was there, that whoever sent me the package believed it as well.

I kept reading:

"Sidney thought these experiments to be both divinely inspired and verifiable by careful observation and study.

"Truth be told, his coterie of German alchemists, disaffected Jesuits who had stolen away monastic tomes from the time of Charlemagne, and troubadours from Toulouse all looked to Sidney for moral guidance and an extended patronage from his Queen. There was a sense, for Sidney, that he could heal the divisions between Papists and Protestants that had ravaged Europe, finding a common religious experience based on celestial song.

"However, these experiments could not be kept from prying enemies forever. A rival secret society who called themselves Devolutionaries—mostly from those under the employ of Hapsburg Spain and Austria, but also the French, who were greatly angered by Sidney's presence in Holland and were fearful that the English meddling could spread—began to plot a thwarting of Aeropagus. Their sigil was the bear, one of the few natural enemies of the porcupine, which happened to be prominent in the coat of arms of the Sidneys.

"The battle at Zutphen, which caused Sidney's death, then, was orchestrated purely to slay Sidney and to crush English advancements in magical poetics. A murder by poison or knife would have been too conspicuous. Spanish armies, then, had to be set into motion. With bitter irony, the Devolutionaries knew full well that Sidney was gallant and also foolhardy, and would not hesitate to rush into battle to save a lost cause. His English forces vastly outnumbered, he charged forward. However, the Devolutionaries had paid a Dutch squire three Spanish florin to steal Philip's armour. He was able to steal the leggings. Had it not been for this theft, Sir Philip Sidney might have survived. It was easy for the English to spread the rumour that Philip had spurned his leggings in order to rush into the battle in all haste. Thus after his long, agonising death, the Aeropagus society was doomed. He had written one final, secret poem on his deathbed, but it has been lost to time."

I had no way to verify any of these claims, but it was the one true thread I could find, and I held onto it for dear life.

When I was finished with reading the monograph, and dawn was breaking, I decided to bite the bullet with the third file on the disk. I should have slept. Instead I read.

The third file didn't begin with the passenger at all, but with me. This story began with me driving down a narrow state highway. I was squinting ahead. On the seat next to me was a manila envelope with a Minneapolis postmark and a return address that said "Aeropagus Storage" with an address. I noted to myself that I was desperate to try to finish the story about the passenger (which was only paraphrased in this version). I was in dire straits. It was becoming all too much for a story. I recalled the shock and thrill I had received when I had received the envelope, and I looked down at my seat at it. The envelope didn't have my address, only my name.

I found myself going to one of the suburbs around the outskirts of the airport. It was noted in the story that it was late at night, an hour or two before midnight. I drove on winding roads, until I made a gentle turn down a hill. Warehouses were on either side of me. This was the place. As I was about to pull into the parking lot of the warehouse to my left, I saw a horse hobble across the road right in front of my car. I swerved. The horse disappeared into the scrawny woods on the other side of the warehouse.

There was a car coming toward me in the other lane, which I tried to avoid. In the story, I had a feeling of both emotional distance and stoic certainty regarding what was happening. I felt the shock of the vibration of steel, the desperate turning of the steering wheel. I stepped on the brakes. The instants were elongating but, in the end, they were just instants, and it was too late. I had no control. The car slid forward—I couldn't tell if I clipped the other car, or the other way around. But I was the one who stopped the car, and the other kept moving, sidewinding down the road. My

Corolla was only grazed, but I had a sharp stiffness in my neck. I opened the door and hobbled out to inspect the damage.

Then I saw the third car coming toward mine, fast.

This car did not slam the brakes as it hit my car. The Corolla was pushed over the side of the embankment. My trunk popped open, and hundreds of sheets of dot-matrix paper spilled out.

The other car put itself in reverse, and skidded backward from the berm.

When it stopped, I ran toward it, waving my hands, hysterical, cursing. The windows were tinted black. I moved to knock on the windows, but something stopped me. The car was silent except for its own engine.

I took a few steps back, and then the car revved and was soon out of sight.

I picked up a few of the stray pieces of paper that had scattered onto the road. They all had different versions of the same story. My story. I read patches:

"The passenger was looking for stories to resuscitate . . ."

"He drove away, not sure whether his family would be able to forgive him . . ."

"The passenger drove his car into the reinforced steel partition of the warehouse, desperate to get inside . . ."

"The Order of the Lamb assented . . ."

I had no doubt that it would keep going.

I looked up and saw the faint tail-lights of an airplane above me. The airplane was making its descent into the airport. It might have been the same plane as it always was, or a different one. Even if the same things were happening, they would mean something different every time.

My body was still aching from the slightest movement, but I scurried down the embankment, which wasn't as steep as I thought it was. When I went into the driver's side to turn off the ignition, I startled, because I realized with a rush that this Corolla was not mine.

There were lots of green Corollas on the road, and there were many times when I'd find myself trying to open someone else's car door with my keys. This was similar, though on a far vaster scale. The car was indeed nearly identical to my own, but not completely so. There were little touches that kept rising to the surface of my perception—the "1" button on the stereo that was scuffed a little on my Corolla was not; the window sticker pass for Minnesota State Parks was for 1999 and not 2000; the stain on the upholstery of the passenger's seat was a couple inches lower than it should have been.

I wondered, then, whose car this was—and moreover, why I was driving it.

I was about to call Kristin on my cell, but searched my pockets. No phone. I went back to the car and searched all the nooks of the car that wasn't quite my own, but no phone. Then it dawned on me that it was, in fact, 1999 and I wasn't supposed to have a cell phone.

Wandering up from the embankment in a crouch, worn to the bone, I made my way to the warehouses. This was the address that I had been sent, and the paranoia about the two cars that had collided with me was more of an afterthought. What was I supposed to be doing there? I tried the door of the first warehouse but it didn't open. I then happened to look at my keyring, which I had been clutching since the collisions, before I was going to put it in my pocket. There was a key on there that I didn't recognize. Just a normal key. I slid it into the lock and turned. The interior was vast and dark, except for blue circular lights that shone in a slow crawl throughout the space. Bright and revealing nothing. There were also red curtains, acting as capes on invisible bodies, flowing toward me. And I could hear a song, in the distant recesses of the warehouse.

What was the warehouse holding? The warehouse was holding the song, the song that I had always longed to hear, but never could, because I was always too busy and too distracted with my own pains and insecurities. Like verses encased in lines—the hard forms of meter and rhyme—the music and the words were kept from the world inside these walls. This was Philip Sidney's poem of dying, his lost last poem.

This was the story—I was listening to this song, at last. And I was there, and I was never to leave.

And yet, this is not the end . . .

In the second warehouse, it is completely dark. An antiphon of nothing-to-see. Then, a small square of orange light, flashing. The printer is out of ink. The paper, filled with The Words, has no light to reflect against it.

Footsteps. The opening of a machine. Ejection. Black fluid on unseen fingers. A shaking of a cylinder. Then a clicking shut. Everything in place. The whirring begins again, like a mechanical bird pecking at wood. The paper spools to the floor. Every twenty minutes or so, hands tear off a sheaf and place it into a manila envelope, sealing the envelope with a gummy tongue. Although it's hard to discern the unilluminated dimensions of the warehouse, the envelope is walked to the other end and put into a slot, which leads to a disorganized back office, sealed off from the rest of the warehouse.

Here, in a room no bigger than a closet, there is a single overhead light in a socket. As soon as the envelope falls through the slot (with no light being emitted to the other side),

. . . I begin addressing it to you. I have been in here a long time. My need is great. I am going to die when you die. Who am I? I am part of you. The Words are Your Words, the totality of whatever you will say and think and write.

Alan, when you were a child, there was so much terror. So much. This was the reason you began to write, to make stories out of the things you could see. It was a way to make limitations out of the world. This was your Aeropagus, in the pencils clutched in your first-grade, sinister hand.

Things grew, you grew, and the terror became admixed with desire—and more than a desire not to be terrified. You wanted better things. You wanted people to admire you and your imagination. This was, this is, your Philip Sidney Game. Always thirsty. Always carted off from the battlefield but angling for water. So how do you signal? How do you let the knight-of-water inside of you know of your thirst?

Here in this story, Sir Philip Sidney is only a phantasm. The devolutionaries are an illusion as well—they are you, they are what you use to thwart your semblance of inner peace. They are in constant battle with what you want to create. It is a wide-ranging battle across many places of your life and over nearly all your years. You didn't begin that story twelve years ago. You only began it this year, but its aims to show how you lived twelve years ago are true, and how much you are trying to be true is true. Though it's nothing to be afraid of, one day

it will be finished. All the threads will weave
together and the warehouse doors thrown open,
and the office park of plasterboard and glass
will sink into the untouched wetlands, and
the passenger will board his plane for home.
Then it will be finished. God willing,
when you are at the end of your life, you
might come across this story in an old
ancient stick of memory, and with
your eyes creased with those necessary heart-
aches countless, you will read it and allow
the story enter into you once more,
and for a moment it will be your life
before you take your last breath, and you let
the horse lead you into the woods of May.

Acknowledgments

Grateful acknowledgment is made to the following publications and anthologies in which some of these stories first appeared: *Strange Horizons* ("Tyrannia"); *Spolia* ("A Rendition"); *Blue Penny Quarterly* ("Cudgel Springs"); *Interfictions 2*, ed. by Christopher Barzak and Delia Sherman ("The Warp and the Woof"); *Logorrhea*, ed. by John Klima ("Plight of the Sycophant"); *Caketrain* ("Dancing in a House"); *Asimov's Science Fiction Magazine* ("Walking Stick Fires," "The Flowering Ape," "The Wildfires of Antarctica"); and *Interfictions Online* ("The Philip Sidney Game"). "Moonlight Is Bulletproof" was published as a standalone ebook by Weightless Books.

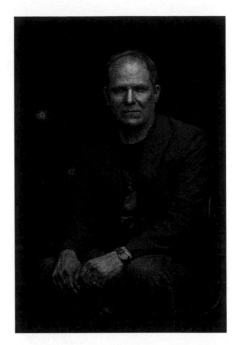

About the Author

Alan DeNiro (alandeniro.com) was born in Erie, Pennsylvania. He graduated from the College of Wooster with a B.A. in English and the University of Virginia with an M.F.A. in creative writing. He is the author of the story collection *Skinny Dipping in the Lake of the Dead* and the novel *Total Oblivion, More or Less*. His short stories have appeared in *One Story*, *Asimov's*, *Santa Monica Review*, *Interfictions*, and elsewhere. He lives outside of St. Paul, Minnesota with his wife Kristin Livdahl and their twins, Ally and Toby.